Simon

-|-

Tyler G. Mower

ISBN 978-1-7378148-0-1
ISBN 978-1-7378148-2-5 (pbk)
ISBN 978-1-7378148-1-8 (ebook)

Cover art by: Tyler G. Mower
Edited By: BookHelpLine.com

To my beloved parents
Nann & Doug Mower

*"For the Lord seeth not as man seeth;
for man looketh on the outward appearance,
but the Lord looketh on the **heart**."*

1 Samuel 16:7

Acknowledgements

This novel would never have come into existence without the diligent support, encouragement, and assistance of my wonderful mother. She trudged through each draft helping with the never-ending adjustments and edits needed.

I must express my gratitude to the many friends and neighbors who eagerly read through the manuscript and provided feedback and suggestions to help bring the story to life. You know who you are.

A special thanks to my grandmother whose poetic talent not only enhanced the story but created the perfect bookend. Though she loved the story, I hope she is now getting a personal account of it!

To the staff at BookHelpLine who edited the novel to free it of a myriad of grammatical errors and ensure consistency throughout the book. If any errors remain, they are on account of myself.

To my wife who supported me through who knows how many evenings typing, editing, adjusting, expanding, and thinking through the story.

Lastly, to you the reader. Thank you for taking the time to read this story. Though this is a work of fiction I have sought to be true to the events, locations, and the pivotal character described. I purposefully left out descriptions of pretty much all other characters in hope that as you read it, you put yourself, your loved ones, friends, and enemies into the story that perhaps it will become more personal to you. That being said, it is a story where the heart of the characters is far more important than their appearance.

If your journey through this story moves you as much as the process of creating it has for me, then all the challenges and frustrations of completing it will have all been worth it. I hope you enjoy.

Preface

The four biblical accounts of Christ's crucifixion are given to us in Matthew chapter 27, Mark 15, Luke 23, and John 19. When the four are read side-by-side, differences in the timeline and details of the hectic events leading to and around Golgotha are evident. I took some liberties in the timeline of that day to organize them in a way that was beneficial for this story.

For myself, the differences in the four gospel accounts are of no concern. The important fact is we have their testimony. As brutal as Christ's crucifixion was, it culminated in the completion of the first half of the atonement when He declared, "It is finished." Shortly thereafter His atonement for all mankind; men and women; bond and free; young and old; past, present, and future inhabitants was made complete as he rose from the tomb breaking the bands of death.

Let us seek to honor Him, by partaking of the atonement He personally made for each one of us. Through Him, we overcome our shortcomings as we strive to live what he taught, are cleansed from our sins as we repent, are healed of our pains and sorrows as we turn to Him, and ultimately overcome death as we too will rise from the grave because of Christ's victory over all these mortal frailties.

Finally, I deliberately chose to use the Savior's title and name Christ twice in the text of the novel. Since this is a work of fiction, I did not want to overuse His sacred name.

Simon

Prologue

-|-

Day Of
Friday, April 3—8:10 am

A minute passed. The next few hours he knew would alter his life. This fact seared into his soul. It was a gut feeling, an instinct that filled his being. Change within him had already begun. He was now a different man than when he had awakened. He knew this because of the situation he was in and the gaze that was searching his soul.

Their presence had never been shared; their eyes had never met. Though turmoil surrounded them, in this moment the commotion vanished. The pressing crowd, the noisy city, and dust all melted away. Nothing remained but the small patch of ground where they stood.

He became incredibly self-conscious. Not of his clothing or appearance, but of his character. No longer was he sure of himself, who he was, his purpose in life, or the work he held so important. The concerns and duties of the day fled from his mind. All that remained was the uncomfortable gaze. Those eyes made him agitated and desirous to flee. He wished he could fade into the crowd and become an insignificant individual among the throng.

No glance had ever caused him to question so much about

himself. Entering his eyes, it expanded to his mind and heart. It filled his being. It uncovered his secrets, revealed his intentions, found his faults, and understood his opinions, desires, hopes, and dreams. Somehow these were unlocked and shared without a word being said. This left him feeling vulnerable and exposed. There was nothing he could hide behind. No lie or deception could mask his inner conscience. Everything about him was an open book.

Strangely, he felt calm. The initial worry of being so completely understood was replaced by wonder. He longed to know how, through a simple look, so much information was revealed about himself. Further, he was shocked to find gratitude bridging the gap between their eyes. It made no sense. More curious still: without a spoken word he was being strengthened; not physically, but emotionally and mentally. It was like his whole being was broken down piece-by-piece and then put back together, stronger than it had been before.

He did not know what the outcome of this situation would be. The day, which had begun hopeful and bright, had turned incredibly bleak. Yet, in the eyes that stared at him, he saw peace and kindness. A faint flame of hope flickered inside. Somehow everything would be okay.

Chapter I

-|-

Morning Of
Friday, April 3—5:30 am

Simon awoke before the rising of the sun. The darkness of night had not fully lifted, and bright stars remained visible while fainter orbs had faded from view.

Simon sat up on his ground cloth, which doubled for both bed and blanket. Next to him lay his satchel. Out of a front pocket, he took a wrapped bundle. Inside were three small cakes he had received the day before. He set the food down in front of him, carefully unwrapping the cloth. With the food open to the morning air, Simon gave thanks for the coming day, the rest he had received, the meager meal, and the hands that had prepared it.

Each bite was like eating flour, it dried his mouth of all saliva making it difficult to swallow. Thankfully, his water pouch was full and a gulp of the cool liquid between each bite assisted in transporting the morsels to his belly. What the cakes lacked in taste they made up for in nutrients. They gave him the energy needed to complete the last leg of his journey.

Simon anticipated a full and plentiful meal at the inn where he had arranged to stay for the next few nights. The meals of the inn made the food he now ate seem like fodder for pigs. The innkeeper spared no expense on the meals he provided, a good recompense for the cost of his accommodations. For the time being, Simon sat silently in the dull twilight, grateful for the sustenance he had.

Two biscuits consumed, he rewrapped the third and returned it to the front pouch of his satchel. A traveler, after all, must prepare for the unexpected. Who knows when an extra piece of food will come in handy?

The food filled his body with energy, giving strength to his muscles, and fully waking him from his sleep. He tied his sandals to his feet, then stood and shook the dirt and sand from the ground cloth. Folding and tightly rolling it, he carefully stuffed it into the central pouch of his satchel. In doing so, he was wary not to crease the contracts he hoped to have signed by the end of the day. He then slung the straps of both his satchel and water pouch over his shoulder and set out for the day.

Simon descended the narrow decline of the small natural amphitheater where he had stayed the night. At its mouth, he turned and peered into the protective cove. He was struck with gratitude for having discovered it years ago. It provided a safe and protected enclosure in which to spend the night. Over the years he had never found traces of other people using it. For this reason, he considered it perfectly safe, a shelter from storms, and a hiding place from robbers.

On one of his first travels to the region, as night had descended over the land, Simon had frantically sought a protected place where he could sleep. He had underestimated the time it would take to arrive at his final destination. Knowing night travel made him an easy target for thieves, he left the road and looked for shelter among the crags and rocks.

He walked along the bed of a dry creek, which forked multiple times into smaller branches. One tributary descended from a plateau above. Considering it better to be higher than lower, Simon scrambled to the top. Upon breaching the crest of the plateau, he found the area barren of trees and shrubs but covered in a blanket of short wild grasses and sprinkled with vibrant yellows of the White Mustard, purple and white of the Crown Anemone, and the heaven pointing Blue Lupin.

In the dimness of the fading light, he noticed a hill near the center of the plateau. He walked toward it, hoping to find some stone outcropping or alcove that would provide shelter. From time to time, he stopped and listened, more from paranoia than anything else, in an effort to detect any sounds that might indicate others in the vicinity. All he heard was the silence of the landscape.

As he approached the hill, it appeared to be nothing more than a mound of dirt being slowly eroded by the rains and winds of time. To his surprise, he found a narrow slit on the backside of the hill, wide enough to walk through. He entered the gap, which inclined toward the center of the hill. After a few steps, the passage opened up into a small natural bowl. The bottom was nearly level and consisted of fine dirt. On the side opposite the entrance were two nearly flat slabs of stone. These boulders had settled with one overlapping the other, creating a triangle gap between them. Simon crouched down and surveyed the shallow cavern. He removed a few rocks and clumps of dirt, spread out his blanket, knelt and gave thanks for having found the shelter, and petitioned divine protection as he slept. Then he lay down, closed his eyes, and rested from the labor of the day.

Over the years, Simon returned to this spot every time he ventured this way. It had become as familiar to him as his home. He had taken time to flatten out the cavern floor with dirt and sand. He also hollowed out some of the dirt between the boulders so his whole body could fit under their protective roofing.

Three years after having found the cove, as he reached the entrance passage, he audibly said, "Hello my little inn." From that day the name had stuck.

— — —

On this bright and peaceful morning, Simon exited his little inn through the narrow gap. He turned left around the outside of the hill, walked along the lip of the plateau, descended a steep tributary to the creek bed below, and made his way toward the road. He was mindful to return by a different path than the one used to get to his inn. Though his frequency here was not enough to create a permanent path, Simon did not want to leave obvious tracks leading to his safe haven. Such a tragedy would undoubtedly lead others to find his abode under the stars. If others knew its location, it would compromise his safety in staying there.

He always made sure no one was around when he left the road in the evening. In the morning, he made sure to get an early start so he could reach the road before it was littered with travelers. So far, his precautionary strategies had worked in his favor.

Reaching the road, Simon turned and walked southeast. The air was cool and fresh. The fragrance of the earth, sweet. A clear sky lay overhead with only the morning star visible in the heavens. Birds sang their cheerful songs as they fluttered around the rocks and plants of the landscape.

On such a beautiful morning, Simon felt his life could not be more blessed. He felt confident in his business goals for the day. The contracts he carried would ensure five years of prosperous trade and expansion east. He recognized the success he had accomplished and took pride in the amount of wealth achieved. Prosperity allowed him to create a name for himself. There was not a major port or city in the eastern side of the Empire that did not know his name. His amassed riches were far more than he had imagined in his younger years, and now he was determined to see how much he could collect.

A decade earlier, Simon did not possess confidence in himself. Then, every mistake or challenge made him think all was lost. He worried he would not be able to establish a career or provide for a family. He acted tentatively. He did not trust his instincts. As a result, he had been given fewer responsibilities in his apprenticeship. He possessed the ability to succeed, yet he let insecurities and doubts deter him from progressing. He noticed people his age effectively developing their trades, expanding their families, and succeeding in life but he felt incapable of doing the same. In a desperate effort to improve his situation, largely inspired by the faith of his new bride, Simon convinced his master-tradesman to give him the responsibility of leading a caravan. By grace and persistent pleas, he had been entrusted with the task.

Simon learned for himself he could lead men, overcome unexpected circumstances, and take responsibility. After that experience, he walked with confidence, which allowed him to gain respect and trust from his employer, leaders of industry, political officials, and most importantly, his wife. Knowing others believed in him helped Simon's belief in himself to grow.

Over the years, he came to welcome challenges. They filled him with energy and a deep sense of determination. Never again would he let insecurities hold him back from accomplishing something great. This meant most months were spent away from home in pursuit of greater success. He often said his efforts were for his family, but deep down he knew it was for his legacy. His vast wealth allowed him to generously provide for the needs and wants of his family, but the business would be his legacy for his children to carry on.

As he walked, he thought about how he had reached his present circumstance in life. A lot of work, sacrifice, and dedication had gotten him here. The memories of his efforts and success brought a smile to his face.

Many asked if he was so rich and accomplished, why then, did he travel alone without the security and amenities of a caravan? Simon did not think of himself as a gold pincher, but such benefits cost a lot of money. Rather than paying for the added safety of numbers, he invested the funds elsewhere. In so doing, he had the capital to expand his trade faster than others.

The one area where Simon paid well was for information. Never did he embark on a journey without financially pleasing his informants. When he arrived in their towns or cities, his favorite meetings were discussing potential opportunities to expand his realm of influence. Though his business trips had specific objectives and places to be, he was always available for prospecting.

— — —

$\mathbf{H}$e walked at a steady pace. Not fast enough to break a sweat, but brisk enough to be aware of his constant motion. Dust plumed from the impact of his steps on the soft dry road. Already encased in dust, his feet appeared more like dirt than appendages of his body. He was aware of his filthy state, which added to his excitement of getting to the inn where he would be able to wash.

Soon the sun rose above the horizon. Beams of light burst across the landscape. Leaves of plants that dotted the hills and valleys were ignited into vibrant greens. Simon had seen the sun rise on more days than he could remember, but the way the light danced across the landscape this particular morning made him aware of a phenomenon he had never noticed before.

Prior to the sun peeking over the horizon, dirt, stones, and boulders were vivid in color. Their whites, oranges, tans, purples, blacks, and yellows were distinctive in the flat light of dusk, each color clamoring for attention. In contrast, plants, especially leaves and grasses, were a uniform dark green. Now in direct sunlight, dirt, stones, and boulders became more uniform, while the plants and flowers became distinct and vibrant in color. The adage, to look at something in a different light, struck him as a profound piece of sagacity.

"How great the wisdom of our maker," he mused, "to give each creation its own time to shine."

The farther he walked, the more his mind began to wander, consider, question, and ponder. He was influenced by the circumscribed points of his surroundings, past experiences, and future hopes and dreams. Thoughts, after all, are easily ignited by the boredom of lengthy walks, and they also flow like a meandering river.

"I'll arrive and go directly to the inn," thought Simon. "With luck, before midday, I'll be cleaned up and meeting with the garrison commander, Brutus. I have earned enough favor with him to motivate his efforts to double the force to round up roadside thieves. This should decrease stolen goods by twenty percent. By midafternoon these contracts should be signed, ushering in a new era of growth and expansion. These will make my business the largest in the east and south regions of the Empire. My goodness, the largest producer and distributor of market goods in the region! Ten years ago, I would never have believed I would be in this position. This is going to open additional doors to the north and then on to the west. Think of all the people I will employ. I will be their master. I can't wait to meet them and hear their praises and adoration for being the benefactor of their life. If they're anything like Aelius and his community, prosperity and abundance are assured."

Simon's smile broadened even wider at the memory of meeting Aelius and his village, just days before. "I cannot wait to see him again. I believe he is a kindred friend. Together we will fill each other's purses to bursting!"

He also reflected on the beauty of the land around him. There was something about the rolling hills, the light-colored rocks, the way trees grew on hillsides, desert flowers, chirping birds, and the fresh fragrant air that made him think of carefree childhood days.

Then he reminded himself to refer to the hills as mountains

when talking with the locals. Last year he had added a few cities in Greece, including Katerini, to his trade routes. He had seen the legendary mountain of the Gods, Mount Olympus, and learned for himself what a mountain really was. Such a monstrous mass of earth dwarfed anything in this region. But the inhabitants of the area took pride in their mountains, and Simon knew well the necessity of complimenting things people held dear, if for no other reason than earning their trust.

Thinking of comparisons between different regions, the distances between them, and about his travels to far-off locations, Simon caught himself counting his steps.

"148, 149, 150."

This jarred his concentration. He did not know when he had started counting steps, but it had been at least a hundred and fifty steps back.

"I have more important things to think about than the number of steps I take." Whereupon he began rehearsing his sales pitch for the first contract he hoped to have signed that day.

As the morning wore on, the road became busy. At each intersection, the traffic doubled. Eventually, the people departing the nearby city were as numerous as those trying to reach it. The air became extremely dusty making breathing a challenge.

Many brought goods from far locations to barter and sell. Some groups took up nearly the entire width of the road with their extravagant caravans, forcing people traveling in the opposite direction onto the shoulder.

Locals from surrounding regions herded their best flocks to the great temple in honor of the feasts and festivities. Some gave up trying to keep their animals together among the throng and instead guided them in the rough terrain paralleling the road.

Boisterous conversations ensued, stemming from the mingling of locals and travelers of distant lands. Some debated political or religious topics, seeking to show their intellect. A few loudly countered opposing opinions. Others simply nodded their heads in agreement, even though they found the opinions of others off the mark, radical, or trivial. The only evidence of their disagreement was in the glazed look in their eyes. There were those who wore the face of annoyance. Some wanted peace and quiet, an impossible desire in such a crowd. The body language of others indicated their discomfort with being among such a quantity of people. The smells, bodies, animals, and dust, coupled with the clattering of hooves, snorts from beasts of burden, creaking of carts, and multiple conversations were too much. These people remained in silence seeking to block out their surroundings.

With such a fluid throng, there were instances where friends passed and hailed each other joyfully. Apparently, their paths had not crossed for quite some time. Others acknowledged each other as if they saw one another on a regular basis. Then there were the cordial conversations of those who never spent the time to generate a relationship behind the depth of personal walls. A few times, Simon even greeted acquaintances from his business endeavors.

Occasionally, officers on horseback trotted past and expected the masses to give them uninhibited passage. On more than one occasion, their impatient commanding tone rang out, telling everyone to move out of the way. This caused many who had been speaking to hush and wait for the soldiers to pass before continuing their conversations. Despiteful annoyance shone on their faces as progression stopped to make way for the Emperor's troops.

As for Simon, he kept to himself, outpacing the caravans and herding groups. From time to time someone would try to chat with him. Out of politeness, he responded but he only offered the minimum response.

"No, I've been here numerous times."

"Thanks for the advice, however, I already have accommodations."

"Stephen's inn offers the best meals you will find anywhere

in the city. Plus, he is an exceptionally honest man."

"I am here for business, though I will spend some time at the temple."

"I could never move here; it is far too crowded and noisy for my taste."

"I am very far from home."

Simon was not concerned with making friends, especially since the probability of seeing these people again was negligible. Plus, they did not offer an advantage to his work. Those who spoke to him were simply easing the boredom of travel through conversation. Some sparked Simon's interest, but after a few inquiring questions he discovered they posed no leverage for business pursuits. When he recognized this, he gave his regards and continued his brisk pace.

Chapter II

-|-

Day Of
Friday, April 3—7:55 am

Bottlenecked in the narrow street, Simon could not advance faster than the slow pace of the throng. Moments before, he had entered through the western gate via Joppa Road, which was the busiest road in and out of Jerusalem. He had expected jostling and slow progression, however, today was different. The going was even slower than on previous visits. In fact, movement into the city had come to a halt.

The big city always had an exciting energy, especially at this time of year. Passover brought people from regions far and wide to participate in the festivities. Even though it was a somber occasion, the energy and ambiance generated a distinct feeling of celebration. Yells of merchants and consumers, rituals at the temple, the fragrances of incense, the smell of burned sacrifices, the constant mingling of people, all coupled with the presence of soldiers, emissaries, and political officials created a lively hustle. Nevertheless, with the festivities in full swing and Jerusalem at full capacity, Simon felt something was different than on previous visits. Perhaps it was just exhaustion from his long morning walk or his annoyance at being in the midst of the congested horde, but he felt as if life was being sucked from the city.

Up the street near the entrance to the provincial court, he heard what sounded like taunts and yells, but the words were too distant to be understood.

"Probably a dispute over the right to sell on a certain corner or over the rise in prices," he thought.

However, the yells did not dissipate. Rather, they got closer. The muscles in Simon's chest tightened with the sense that something wasn't quite right. His pulse quickened and his eyes seemed to take in more detail. He became uncomfortably aware of his surroundings. The stone walls, shops, and buildings that lined the street created a formidable barrier confining him to the slow pace of the crowd. From behind, people were pushing to get in but up ahead, progression had ceased. He found no solace that he was in the middle of the mass, dead center between the shops and walls that paralleled the road. He had come to a complete stop, standing shoulder to shoulder with those around him.

Claustrophobia set in and he was suddenly overcome by thirst. Having extinguished the last drop of water from his water pouch before entering the city, he had no means to ease his parched mouth.

The sun had risen in the sky and with it came the steady rise in temperature. With everyone packed tightly together, a stifling sensation abounded. This only augmented the stench of body odor with each passing moment. In addition to that nauseating smell was the scent of burned flesh from offerings at the temple and the musky aroma of live animals that dropped their own offerings freely. This all added to Simon's discomfort. The initial excitement of reaching Jerusalem had turned to a loathsome annoyance.

A few minutes passed.

"This is ridiculous," he thought. "Why has movement stopped?"

Impatience crept into his being. He wanted nothing more than to be free of the throng. He tried to push his way forward but this only solicited angry glares, a few curses, and a ripple effect like a wave in water. After a few laborious steps, with his situation unimproved, he consigned himself to waiting.

Ahead, a procession of legionaries slowly approached. Insults and jeers grew in intensity. Simon could make out ten military men. The first was a centurion. Following him were nine soldiers of basic rank. All were jostling to make their way through the thick crowd toward the city entrance.

"The heated taunts must be directed at the soldiers," reasoned Simon. "It is no hidden fact the locals are not pleased with the Empire's presence."

Revolt was a constant concern for Roman leaders. Even though Rome's ability to put down a rebellion was not an issue, their concern was that when one group revolts others are likely to follow. Maintaining peace was essential for the growth of the Empire. Nevertheless, relations here were strained. Israel wanted to regain their independent kingdom. Romans were well aware of this desire and understood how important it was to appease the locals as much as possible. However, this did not keep soldiers and civilians out of small scuffles. Soldiers were known for taking advantage of their military status. Civilians were known for raising prices and offering less than considerate service in return.

Simon wondered at the possibility that this was the first fruits of a revolt.

Standing on his toes, he watched the approaching legionaries. He noticed they seemed to loath their duty. No doubt both sides, soldiers and Israelites, despised each other equally.

The physical effort of pushing through the crowd caused sweat to gather on their foreheads, trickle down past their unlatched helmet straps, and fall from their chins to the dusty ground. They would shout and yell as boisterously as the people around them, the tone of their voices far from a friendly command.

"Move back," yelled one.

"Make room," commanded another.

Aside from these instructions they also let jeers fly.

"They are mocking the crowd as much as the people are mocking them," deduced Simon with a bit of shock.

Never in his travels had he seen such an occurrence. Curiosity now took hold. He struggled to understand why such a tumult was being made.

As the soldiers drew closer, the people in front of Simon started to yell. There was so much noise Simon could not make out entire sentences. He only caught bits and pieces:

"If you be ..."

"... dog."

"We have no ..."

"Filthy wretch ..."

"... save yourself."

"... scum."

"King of ..."

"... Jesus ..."

The words themselves made no sense. However, the feeling of anger and hatred behind them Simon understood.

He instantly felt a need to be away from this place. In the mayhem, he heard the shout of a short but full phrase. Immediately, he stiffened. Fear blanketed him like a dowsing of cold water. As others around him caught the phrase, they too began shouting it in unison.

"Crucify Him, Crucify Him!"

Instinct took control. His feet began moving. He did not care which direction he went, as long it got him away from the scene. He jostled and pushed, trying to make it out of the crowd. He would not be caught in the middle of local issues. Little ground was gained, but at least he was moving.

Angry yells were directed at Simon from those he pushed. Simon did not care. He wanted out and to be uninvolved with whatever evil was afoot. His career and self-image were too important to be tarnished by some local commotion. Simply being present could cause his contacts to question his loyalty and repute, especially if this boisterous group had political or religious qualms.

One final push brought him to the worst of locations. Of all directions he could have gone, Simon bumped into one of the soldiers who continued to curse and command the people to make room.

Chapter III

-|-

Evening Before
Thursday, April 2—5:00 pm

"**S**arah," said Simon, "that was a delightful meal. You make even the bitter foods seem like a royal feast."

"Always a pleasure to have you in our home. I cannot abide the thought of you eating at the local inn, where meals are far too expensive for their meager portions."

"I wish you would allow me to pay for my meal," offered Simon.

He removed some coins from his pouch and placed them near the center of the table.

Sarah just smiled. "You pay us plenty. The industry you bring to our town provides for my family and so many more."

Sarah reached across the low table and pushed the coins back toward him. He reluctantly picked them up and returned them to his pouch.

"Then you must accept my greatest appreciation and thanks for the meal," said Simon.

He turned to retrieve his satchel and water pouch, which had been placed behind his cushion. He swung the straps over his head and rested them on his shoulder.

"You could stay," offered Sarah. "We always worry about you when you sleep under the stars. If you leave early in the morning, you could reach Jerusalem by tomorrow evening."

"One meal is imposing enough. Besides, I desire to get to the city early so I can get everything in order and spend some time at the temple."

"But the roads are no place to spend the night. Robbers are as common today as ever before. Just last week our neighbor, Joshua, was beaten badly on his way home from work. The thieves attacked in broad daylight. Military presence has not stopped such brutal acts."

"I heard. I visited him and his family before coming here. I think he is more upset about his sandals being broken and his cloak torn than the fact that his money and water pouch were stolen. Plus, I think he is a little proud of his black eyes."

"Such attacks are happening more frequently these days," Sarah frowned.

"The cities require our merchandise," Simon replied. "The decrease in sales due to theft is affecting markets. Merchants are concerned and have reported the issue to authorities. I will personally appeal to the garrison in Jerusalem tomorrow. I know the commander, Brutus, well. After years of cultivating a friendship and a side business with him, I am sure I can call in a personal favor. He benefits as much from me, as he does from his own position."

"That will be good, supposing you reach Jerusalem in one piece. Who will protect you between here and there?" challenged Sarah.

"Do not worry. I know the perfect place to spend the night. It is hidden and provides sufficient shelter."

"I still do not agree. You should at least travel with a caravan. There is safety in numbers."

"True. Though they move slow and are plagued with useless

drab talk. I prefer to go at my own pace and let my mind create its own conversations. You learn a lot doing that."

From the first day he had eaten with John and Sarah years ago, she had argued it was best for him to stay the night and leave in the morning. Simon had never known someone who was so honestly concerned about the well-being of others. She believed risk was never worth taking. Secure and safe equaled the best way to live, in her opinion.

Sarah's husband John was one of Simon's first contacts in the region. Simon had been impressed with John from the moment they had met. Since that day, the two had grown so close that if a stranger watched them interact, they would guess they were brothers. Sarah had been so pleased Simon brought work to her husband that she insisted on feeding Simon every time he came through their village. Over the years all of them had become great friends.

As good a friend as she was, Simon would not adhere to her risk-free opinions. It was an argument that occurred every time he stopped by. Experience taught him it was easiest to leave his gratitude for the meal and make his way to the front door. Simon stood and stepped toward the exit.

Sarah grabbed a small bundle of cloth tucked under the low table. "Very well," she said, standing to accompany him to the door. "If you will not stay, take these cakes to give you strength along your way."

Sarah handed him a small, wrapped bundle. He gratefully took the morsels of food and slipped them into the front pouch of his satchel.

"May God watch over and protect you," she said.

"He always does," said Simon as he made his way out of the humble home and into the street. As he walked, he turned around and added with a smile, "Tell John his absence at our meals will not be tolerated. I will stop by on my return trip. I expect to have wonderful news for him."

Chapter IV

-|-

Day Of
Friday, April 3—8:00 am

$\mathbf{H}$e was a strong man. Not like a gladiator or a seasoned soldier, but the kind of strength found in men who know how to work. He was not obese, neither was he lean. He was not tall, nor was he short. By all physical aspects, he was as ordinary as could be. Nothing made him stand out above others. Remove all the cuts, bruises, welts, black eyes, sweat, and dust, and even then, his normal appearance would not cause much attention. No sculptor would choose him as a subject to portray the ideal human. Nor would he be cited as the example of a hideous complexion. Simple plain sandals protected the soles of his feet. His attire was homely. No vibrant colors streaked his cloak, though much of it was stained with fresh and drying blood. Everything about him was simply average.

He stumbled, no doubt from the weight of the wood on his back and the mangled conditions of his body. He put one hand out to brace for the fall, while employing his other in an effort to steady the cross of wood from crushing him. The effort was futile. He fell hard onto his left side, followed by the full weight of the wood on top of him. The momentum of the fall caused his sweat and blood to splatter on the dusty street. He heaved for breath. A single groan escaped his lips, more from the weight of the wood crushing his side than a voluntary expression of pain.

Instantly, the crowd erupted in ecstasy. The man, whose death they desired, had fallen.

His body had barely come to rest on the ground when impatience lashed out like vipers from the soldiers. Their spit, kicks, and whips did not aid in his attempts to rise to his feet. When he got to his knees he was pushed back down by a kick to his waist. He had barely gotten his feet under him again when a whip slicing at his back returned him to his knees.

Exhausted, the man finally stood. He was obviously experiencing intense agony. Dirt and gravel from the road stuck to his bare palms and arms. A smudge of dirt now added its dark color to the crimson on his cheek. The ground where he had fallen displayed smears and streaks of blood.

"Pick up the cross, you maggot," commanded a soldier, pointing intently at the wood.

The man bent down and tried to heave it up but mid-rise, he lost his grip, causing both the cross and himself to topple again to the ground. The cross was too heavy, his body too fatigued to lift it. He lay a moment, mustering the strength to try again.

Again, cheers and laughter erupted.

"You see, he has no real power," yelled a religious leader, which gained approving nods from many nearby.

The soldiers continued their onslaught.

"Stand," ordered the centurion.

"Get up. Get up," demanded the soldier wielding the whip.

Their words, kicks, and lashes could not bring the man to stand or bear the wooden load. They did not seem to acknowledge that it was their own violent actions keeping him from obeying their commands. A kick to his stomach caused him to curl into a tight fetal position, while he gasped for air.

Simon's eyes were fixed upon the man on the ground, while his feet remained planted firmly where he stood. Never had he seen someone so beaten. Even though the man wore clothing, Simon could tell there were multiple unseen wounds beneath. The situation, these people, this man, and the soldiers appalled him.

"Who is he? What crime has he committed to have been sentenced to such a fate? What has he done to deserve the disrespect and hate flung at him?" questioned Simon.

Simon guessed he must be the lowest kind of human—a liar, criminal, thief, murderer, and rebel all rolled into one.

Simon had heard rumors of a man called Jesus, who was from somewhere near Jerusalem. He was supposedly a healer and a great teacher.

"Surely, this man in the dirt is not he. If this is, why would he who does so much good be treated so viciously? This man on the ground must be another. After all, the name Jesus is a common name."

Such a blur filled Simon's mind in an effort to make sense of the scene that he did not notice one of the soldiers take a brisk step to his side. In an instant, Simon was pulled from the crowd and shoved toward the man on the ground. The shock brought Simon to a keen awareness of his surroundings.

For the first time, Simon noticed two other men being led by the soldiers. Unlike Jesus, these men were only carrying a cross beam. Under its weight, they stared at the ground in front of them. Shame for their condemning deeds evident on their faces. Though filthy and showing the signs of having been in prison, they were not beaten and bruised like the man still lying on the ground. Simon instinctively knew, they too were heading to their deaths.

The soldiers directed their impatience toward Simon.

"Carry the cross."

"Pick it up," shouted another.

The mob joined the soldiers. All were now telling Simon

to carry the cross. The legionaries wanted to be done with the mundane execution. The onlookers, pleased Jesus had fallen, were now bored and desired the crucifixion to come swiftly. Though the motivations between the soldiers and crowd were different, they were united in their desire to get moving.

Adrenaline surged through Simon's veins. He quickly scanned for a gap where he could bolt and get away. There was nowhere to go. He was surrounded by the soldiers, boxed in by the throng, and walled in by the street's architecture.

The soldier, who had pulled Simon from the crowd, repeated the command to pick up the cross.

Simon looked at the man lying at his feet. A small stream of blood had made its way across the stone to Simon's right sandal. Shocked by the sight, he quickly moved his foot away. He would not have the blood of a condemned man on him.

Simon had no idea who this man was or what he had done to be doomed to such a fate but carrying the cross for him could jeopardize local business relations. Crucifixion was often served as punishment to enemies of Rome. If this was the case, carrying the cross would make Simon an outcast. Jerusalem was one of his most important hubs. He could not risk losing connections and respect here. Getting this man's blood on him would be his ruin.

Calling out over the mayhem of noise, to bring reason to those around him, Simon yelled, "This is not my affair. I know not this man, nor the crimes for which he has been sentenced. It is unjust for me to be tarnished by his blood."

Immediately, taunts were thrown from angry lips. A rain of spit came down upon him. Simon noticed the soldiers' hands on the hilts of their swords. He wasn't sure if they were going to lash out at the people or him. Their eyes were filled with disgust and contempt. They seemed to detest the horde as much as the crowd hated the man on the ground.

The centurion said something to three soldiers. His message

was concealed from Simon by the boisterous yells all around him.

Instinctively, the three moved to obey. One grabbed Simon by the shoulders and forcefully turned him in the direction of the city gate. In one swift movement, the soldier also removed Simon's satchel and water pouch and flung them to the ground. Two soldiers bent down, lifted the cross, and dropped it on Simon's left shoulder. The weight almost caused Simon's legs to buckle under him. It must have weighed nearly four talents.

The cross was made of coarse, rough wood as if hastily made. Simon felt multiple slivers prick his hands as he gripped and adjusted the cross's weight on his shoulder. A sharp corner dug into his neck. He thought it would sever his shoulder and arm from his body. At least the long vertical beam dragged on the ground, taking some weight off his shoulder.

A cheer from the crowd arose. Never had a cheer filled Simon with such sorrow. He was ashamed of holding the cross and felt his business was ruined. Word would undoubtedly reach his contacts. Worse still was the thought of news reaching his family. How could he ever face them? How could he ever provide for them now? The town would shun him, condemning him and his family to a life of poverty and woe. In a few short moments, his life had completely changed. Bowing his head to avoid looking at anyone, Simon tried to hide underneath the cross. He was now as much an outcast as the man on the ground.

Cheering continued. It was in jubilation that the procession could now proceed.

Simon said to himself, "I might as well be him."

Tears dropped from his eyes and he watched one fall, landing on the dusty street next to the stream of blood that had once again progressed to Simon's feet.

Chapter V

-|-

Five Days Before
Sunday, March 29—8:00 am

He walked briskly in the unexpected cool temperatures of the day. All morning he had not seen a soul on the road, a circumstance that did not occur often. Though, the remote hamlet he had come from could explain the vacancy of pedestrians.

Five days prior, while meeting with one of his informants, a passing comment mentioned a location that could provide quarried limestone. Supposedly, the village had no facilities or sufficient personnel to quarry the stone. Simon's source recommended other sites that had developing infrastructures and more immediate monetary gains but Simon's interest was piqued. He considered the benefits a limestone mine could pose for cities, towns, and vineyards throughout the Empire. Of these, it was the vineyard industry that intrigued Simon the most. The best winemakers paid well for limestone. It was an industry he had not yet exploited but was one that could easily double his business. If providence was on his side, this little piece of information could ultimately lead to major growth and wealth.

Following the meeting with his informant, Simon departed in the direction of the village. After a full day's walk, he arrived.

What he found was little more than shambled homes. None were in pristine repair. Cracks were readily seen in foundations and mortar had fallen from walls, leaving rubble piled at the base of some buildings. A few structures were inadequate for shelter, with roofs that were far from the definition. Some walls appeared as if a mere breeze would topple them to the ground. Yet people resided in such deplorable conditions. At first observance, the hamlet was everything his informant had told him it was. Nevertheless, Simon set about finding the local leader, which did not take long, because he greeted Simon.

"Shalom, fellow brother," said the man from behind. "Are you lost?"

Simon turned to see a lean but strong man striding toward him. His hair was short, mimicking the Roman style, yet it was uneven and a little disheveled. His clothing was thin and worn. It consisted of a Roman toga beneath an open robe that draped from his shoulders to his ankles. Somehow the robe, though well used, had maintained its vibrant blue and tan striped hues.

"Shalom," replied Simon with a pause then added, "Lost? I should think not."

"No stranger comes here without first discovering himself to be lost," said the man.

"My name is Simon of Cyrene. I am interested in the limestone found in this region."

"Forgive my manners, dear friend, I am Aelius. We are not accustomed to strangers in our village. The road ends here and those that get here always seem to be those who have lost their way. If it's limestone you want, there is plenty to be found. But come to my home where you may rest from your journey, eat, and replenish your strength. You will find no better cook than that of my wife."

"I accept," Simon said in his friendliest tone.

Over the next two days, Simon inspected the limestone in the region. He met the inhabitants and observed the potential they had to learn, operate, and maintain a full-scale quarry. Unlike many villages he had visited in the past, Simon saw hope in the eyes of the community—hope for consistent work that would lead to a sustainable and improved life.

That is the strongest kind of hope. It creates results, it drives change, and most importantly, it lays the foundation for success. Simon knew he had stumbled upon a golden opportunity.

On Simon's last night, a communal banquet was prepared as a farewell. It would not have been considered a feast in any of the places Simon currently conducted business. The meal was meager, the portions small, yet it was given in the true meaning of friendship, and to Simon's delight, it was one of the most delicious dinners he had ever eaten.

Before the meal began, Aelius signaled the people to be quiet.

Then, speaking in a loud voice, he said, "Friends and family, we feast this night on behalf of our new friend, Simon. Not only is he a generous and forward-thinking man, but he has also brought hope to our village. I have signed a contract, guaranteeing the limestone in the vicinity be quarried and used on behalf of Simon's business for the following five years. In return, Simon will ensure we receive the facilities and equipment required and will send additional men to direct quarrying efforts."

Everyone burst into cheers cutting off Aelius's final words.

Once the joyful shouts quieted, Aelius added, "Family and friends, you know our path in life has been difficult and uncertain. Many loved ones have left us to pursue a more secure life elsewhere …" He paused, and then with deep emotion said, "Including my two eldest sons, who I have not seen for six years. Simon has offered us the chance to improve our situation, to regain our honor, and make our village flourish."

The contract could not have made Simon more pleased. It opened a new branch of trade and had the possibility of bringing in vast wealth. For the time being, the quarry would employ two-thirds of the community. After five years, if all was going well, Simon promised to offer a new contract that could potentially make this no-name place a common name throughout the Empire.

When Simon left in the morning, the villagers saw him off as if he was their savior.

He had now walked for two hours and had not seen anyone. He was grateful for the solitary circumstance. He reflected on the past few days, those he had met, and the coordination needed to get the quarry up and running. Titus, Simon's right-hand man, would be crucial in organizing the development of the infrastructure, establishing shipping, and maintaining relations.

Clattering to his left snapped Simon out of his thoughts. He looked to see the cause of the commotion. In the distance, a fully packed donkey was quickly approaching. With each leap over a shallow gully or a tight turn around a boulder, goods spilled from the loosening packs tied to its back. Each time its hind quarters came down, the bouncing motion caused merchandise to launch into the air. Simon could easily follow the trail of spilled goods revealing the path where the donkey had run.

Over the crest of a hill in the distance, Simon noticed a man trailing the donkey. Between gasps of breath, the man promised acts of vengeance and curses upon his beast. Perhaps out of fear of his master, or just one of those stubborn moments, the donkey paid no heed to the owner. Rather, with each curse, its pace increased.

The gap between the two steadily broadened. Realizing he would not catch up until the beast had its run, the man started walking up inclines and running down declines. Though winded the man continued to curse.

The donkey's course may have appeared sporadic, but instinct guided its path. Like water, it was following the path of least resistance. By the lay of the land, this would make it cross Simon's path ahead where a broad gully intersected the road.

Simon quickly ran ahead and hid behind a large boulder. His position would conceal his presence. He hoped the donkey would run close enough to him that he could surprise it and catch its lead rope.

From the sound of clanking hooves, Simon knew the donkey would soon come into view. As long as the donkey did not break for the far side of the gully, Simon would be able to head it off. If it went to the other side of the gully, Simon's hiding spot would profit him nothing. He would have to dash out to catch it. This would put Simon in the same situation as the donkey's master, trailing a rampaging beast of burden.

Peeking around the edge of the slab, Simon caught a glimpse of the donkey, and relief flooded him. Thankfully sticking to the path of least resistance, the beast was coming straight toward his location.

A few seconds passed. Simon stood motionless, keeping his presence unknown until the last moment. When the donkey was a few gallops away, Simon quickly stepped forward, blocking its path.

Shouting and waving his arms and hands, Simon caught the full and surprised attention of the donkey. The shock of an unexpected human in front of it caused a moment of hesitation. The donkey back-peddled to avoid running over Simon, sending dirt and rocks flying. With reduced speed, the donkey attempted to redirect its course but in that split second, Simon caught hold of the dangling lead rope. With a firm grip, he pulled down and gained control of the head.

The donkey kicked wildly in an effort to buck free but Simon's grip remained firm. Realizing its efforts were futile, the animal began to settle down.

Gentle words flowed from Simon's mouth, accompanied by soft pats from his free hand on the donkey's neck. Shortly, the beast was as calm and peaceful as the day and Simon could lead it out of the floodplain and back along the road. He directed it to a short stubby tree. Here, on a low branch, he tied the lead rope.

Looking across the landscape, Simon noticed the owner still following his animal's tracks. Simon hollered to get his attention and beckoned for him.

The man was a little confused. He had lost sight of his donkey and thus had not seen the event that had taken place in the gully. Nor had he noticed anyone else in the vicinity. The owner had been so focused on following the donkey's path, he had not seen Simon tie it to the tree.

Squinting, the owner noticed the dark shape of his animal standing in the shade of the tree, and realizing why the stranger was motioning for him, he adjusted his course. As he did, more curses fell across his lips.

Moments later he arrived. He had regained his breath, but the strain of his run was still apparent from the sweat that beaded on his face. His red cheeks testified to either his physical exertion or continued anger.

The man was about sixty years of age. His physical appearance was that of one who had maintained a strong healthy lifestyle. Nevertheless, having reached later years of life, his energy limits were not what they had been. He stood slightly shorter than Simon. His full beard was streaked with gray. His tan leathery skin attested to a life of work in the sun.

As he approached, the donkey went into another anxious fit. It kicked and tugged at the rope, trying to break free. The tree shook and quaked as though it might be yanked from the ground, however the roots did not pull free, the firm branch did not give, and the knot in the rope held fast.

Without acknowledging Simon, the master glared at the beast and yelled, "I'll feed you to the buzzards." This incited the donkey to again tug and yank on the rope.

"Perhaps a gentler command would have a better effect," offered Simon.

For the first time, the master acknowledged the stranger, yet he did not introduce himself. Rather he began ranting.

"This animal brings nothing but frustration." Motioning across the landscape, he added, "Just look at my goods. It will take hours to gather it all. Half of it is probably ruined. This beast has cost me more than it was worth."

Exasperated, he continued, "Even after I gather it, separate out what is still good, and repack everything, the day will be far spent. Due to this animal, I am already two days behind schedule."

Simon, himself feeling pressed on time, internally reasoned, "I must not get haggled into helping this man further. I have done service enough. I have places to be and commitments to keep. I am well above the trinket goods he has to offer. No doubt he could not compensate me for assisting him."

The owner was at his wits' end. Frustrated and tired, his shoulders drooped and a slow, deep exhale was released from his chest. The man's eyes were devoid of hope for his future.

The desperation Simon saw in the man brought to his memory an experience he'd had decades before. It had not crossed his mind for as long as he could remember. He wondered how he had ever forgotten it. He smiled at the memory as if he was reliving it. What joy it brought to his own heart. In an instant, a deep sense of empathy for this man came over him and he felt impressed to share his experience.

Surprising himself Simon said, "Worry not my friend. I will help gather the strewn supplies."

"What concern is it to you?" said the man in a harsh, unbelieving manner. "I owe you nothing, nor can I pay you for your service."

"This is true. But to walk past someone in need and offer no assistance is the act of a coward."

The words tasted bitter in Simon's mouth. He could not believe he had said them. However, it seemed the right thing to say, even though it did not represent his philosophy, for he had often looked the other way when passing those in need. He considered them the responsibility of others.

"You have already helped a great deal by capturing this beast," the man said as he glared at the donkey. Then, looking at Simon, in an uncertain and questioning tone he added, "Yet, you offer additional assistance. What is it you want of me?"

Slowly, as if trying to understand himself, Simon said, "Only to help."

"Come now, no stranger pauses in his journey for another these days. Who are you?"

"Simon of Cyrene. Like yourself, I am a man of business."

"A man of business indeed," the man said mockingly. "Yet you carry no goods or merchandise."

"That is not my role."

Simon transitioned the conversation, "In whose presence do I have the pleasure of being?"

The man was swayed by the amiable and genuine manner in which Simon asked this question, and replied, "Timothy of Sychar."

Then, more to himself, as if to convince himself that Simon must be a heaven-send, he said, "People these days walk past those in need."

Hearing this, Simon confirmed his non-angelic status. "The actions of others do not determine my own. An experience I had years ago bids me to stop and help a fellow brother."

Simon then began to tell his tale. Timothy listened intently.

"Years ago, for my last task before completing my apprenticeship, I was put in charge of a small caravan. I was entrusted with my master's products, to barter and sell through towns and cities all the way to Jerusalem. The journey was a success. I managed to sell all the merchandise and with the profits, purchased needed items to ensure the success of the following season. Among the items bought was a large quantity of wood, with which my master was going to expand his storehouse.

"We experienced an unusually rainy day outside of a village called Nazareth. One of the carts, laden with wood, slipped off the road. The driver managed to keep the cart from tumbling down a hillside. Nevertheless, the weight of the shifting wood against the cart's grates caused the sides to break, spilling the cargo of wood down the slope.

"A quick assessment revealed no one had been injured. Turning our attention to the cart we found the wheel and axle had been damaged beyond repair.

"Being late in the day, I ordered the train to continue to our designated encampment. They were to establish camp, secure the supplies for the night, unload one of the remaining carts, then come back to load the strewn wood. A few men remained with me to salvage what we could and prepare the wood for when the other cart returned.

"As the rest of our group pushed forward, we set about gathering the scattered wooden planks. The situation worsened as we found many had splintered, twisted, and snapped among the boulders and rocks.

"I was at a loss. I envisioned this one event ruining my future. My master would deem me unfit to start my own practice. It was his endorsement that would enable me to commence my own trade. I saw years of labor, learning, and preparation melting away into oblivion. I would never be entrusted with responsibility again. Heavy despair filled my soul. I felt glum and depressed. My emotions mirrored the scene of rain that poured from the gray and black clouds above.

"The men who had stayed with me were as stricken as myself. Our master was known for his strict discipline. Others had been discharged for smaller issues than this. He demanded perfection.

Errors were a sign of weakness and incompetence.

"I could follow the example of my master and discharge the responsible driver yet I knew when I returned, my master would discharge me. It was not improbable that he would dismiss the entire group, saying, 'A true leader would never entrust cargo to the hands of an incompetent driver. And worthwhile employees would not follow such a foolhardy leader.'

"My mind raced through all the worst-case scenarios, all of which led to me being sent to the streets, disgraced, and broken.

"I reviewed my actions and decisions leading up to the accident, all of which seemed to support a bitter end. I had chosen the wagon driver who ruined the load of wood. I had decided to try to make up time and pushed the caravan on in rainy conditions when we should have stopped. My desire to impress my master seemed to have blinded my judgment. Because of me, all were in this horrible situation. I figured I would be relieved of my apprenticeship, as well as the men that would follow such a leader as myself. I could not figure out how to ensure all our careers. The men looked to me for what to do and I looked to the sky, through drops of rain, hoping for some guidance on the matter.

"At that moment, a young man of about fifteen came around a bend in the road. He noticed the cart still tilted precariously on the hill and surveyed the splintered grates, broken wheel, and axle as he approached.

"I was standing near the growing piles of wooden planks. One was for undamaged wood, the second for the planks that were splintered and broken. The young man walked up to me and inquired if he could be of assistance.

"Replying sarcastically, I said, 'Only if you have an extra cart and spare wood.'

"The young man said nothing in reply.

"He seemed to be deep in thought. After a moment he said, 'I will return.'

"Briskly he turned and went back the same way he had come.

"I dismissed him as a lad who simply wanted to see the wreckage and I set about helping my men gather the wood. To my dismay, within an hour, the young man returned driving a smaller cart. I stood to the side as he reigned the single donkey to a halt next to me. With a huge grin of kindness, he descended from the cart's seat. He walked straight up to me and said, 'I would like to trade this cart,' motioning to his own cart, 'for your cart.'

"I stood open-mouthed, thinking the lad was not right in his head. In my silence, he bettered the deal.

"He beckoned me closer to his cart. Neatly laid in the back was a pile of wooden planks.

"'I would also like to trade these for the broken pieces of wood in your pile.'

"I gaped at the young man, questioning what sane human would make such an exchange. Within his eyes, I saw he understood my situation, my fears, and my concerns. It was as if he had been told my life's story. I stared at him, not out of the absurdity of his offer, but because of the understanding I saw in him. At that moment, I knew he fully intended to follow through with his deal. His motives were simply to help.

"I must have shown my gratitude and acceptance, because he stated, 'Then we are agreed.'

"Quietly, almost reverently I told the young man, 'I am indebted to you.'

"He said calmly, '*All* are in need of help.'

"I considered that short phrase to be nothing more than a few words."

Simon paused in his story and was pensive. Audibly, though obviously more to himself than to Timothy, he asked, "How could I have forgotten that?" He seemed to finally comprehend the lesson he had been taught that day long ago.

Simon looked at Timothy and continued, "So, when I'm observant enough to notice, I strive to help where I can. I see you could use some help. And who knows, perhaps someday you will help me."

For the first time since Simon began his story, Timothy spoke. His temperament had settled. He was now grateful that Simon had stopped to assist.

"I am indebted to you Simon of Cyrene. I thank you for your service."

Putting his hand on Timothy's shoulder, Simon said, "Now, let us gather your merchandise."

Chapter VI

-|-

Day Of
Friday, April 3—8:05 am

The wood's weight pressed painfully into Simon's shoulder. Its awkward distribution forced Simon to hunch forward, fatiguing his entire body. A precarious balance was required to keep the cross from tilting side to side while maintaining standing stability. Balancing the cross was one difficulty, keeping his grip was another.

Smeared with Jesus's blood, the cross was both slippery and sticky. The scent filled Simon's nose and his stomach churned in a bout of nausea. Simon continually readjusted the placement of his hands to maintain his grip but each time he moved his hands, the cross rolled to the side causing splinters to wedge into his skin.

Blood quickly covered his palms and smeared on his clothing. He knew these stains would ruin his reputation. His business in Jerusalem would never recover from the disgrace of this moment. Though the amount of blood on him was relatively little, he felt as if he had been doused in it.

Simon hefted the cross from his left shoulder over his head and repositioned the beam on his right. For some reason, it seemed more natural to place the cross on his right shoulder.

"Move dog," shouted one of the soldiers, confirming in Simon's mind that in just a minute, he had fallen from his social standing to the bottom tier of society.

This made the crushing weight of the cross feel twice as heavy; it was both a physical and emotional burden.

The dead weight of the cross was physically draining. Simon figured Jesus must have carried it from Pilate's court. Though the judicial grounds were not far away, Simon was filled with a sense of awe at how someone in such a condition, beaten as he was, could even stand, let alone carry a cross this far.

Glancing down, Simon looked at Jesus who was still lying on the ground. To his surprise, Jesus raised himself onto his hands and knees. The motion was slow and labored yet determined with a level of energy that was unexplainable.

Reaching with his right hand, Jesus gripped a fold of Simon's robe. Simon felt the tug as Jesus used the fold to steady himself while he rose. Twice more Jesus grabbed Simon's clothing as he came to a standing position.

The effort expended to rise was expressed in Jesus's exhausted face. For a brief second, he closed his eyes as if internally searching for the strength to continue. His mouth was open as he quietly gasped for air.

Simon had never seen a face so tired, yet so powerful. The juxtaposition of those expressions was so shocking that he stood in silence, staring at Jesus while two thoughts battled in his mind.

The first told him to throw the wood down, move back into the crowd, and disappear from the scene. After all, he did not know this man nor the crime he was being punished for; therefore, it was not his duty to carry this man's cross.

"Why should I be disgraced? There are others who are eager for his death. They should be the ones to carry his cross. Any of them are just as capable of carrying it as I am."

Simon doubted anyone in the procession held positions of

influence as important as his own, which led him to think, "Much better for them to be disgraced than myself."

But his second thought was of wonder.

"Who is this man? How is it he is so strong after being so brutally beaten? Only one with a virtuous personal character could carry himself so magnificently in such a situation. He does not yell back at the soldiers or multitude. He does not openly whine or moan. He does not ask to rest or point out his battered condition. He does not look at the people with revenge or hate. In contrast, the other two condemned men in the procession are doing all of these."

Simon was torn between wanting to run away and his curiosity at this man, Jesus. Interest to better understand him kept Simon in his place, even though all his logic was screaming at him to flee. Amid his mental war, an inexplicable moment transpired between Simon and Jesus.

Slowly turning his head and opening his eyes, Jesus met Simon's gaze. Simon noticed, in detail, the man's face dripping with sweat and blood, smeared with dirt, covered in bruises and cuts, and an expression of complete exhaustion. Both eyes were black, but his left was nearly swollen shut. Never had Simon seen a face so pain-stricken.

When their eyes met, the turmoil around them vanished. Though the crowd and soldiers were surrounding them, their insults melted into silence, leaving as it were, Jesus and Simon alone on a vacant street. Even the weight of the cross became insignificant. The former rays of the sun now felt like an enveloping warmth.

Their eyes remained locked. No words were spoken; nevertheless, an entire transfer of information crossed the bridge of their gaze. Simon felt his soul being searched. His secrets were unlocked, motives known, and character understood. There was nothing he was able to keep hidden. The nooks, crannies, and corners of his mind were unrolled like scrolls.

Simon did not see hate, disgust, shame, regret, or accusation in the eyes of Jesus. To his surprise, he saw perfect love, kindness, understanding, and compassion. Simon did not glean nearly the same amount of information about Jesus, as Jesus gained from him.

Instinctively, Simon knew Jesus was good and kind. He also knew he was innocent of the crime for which he had been condemned.

Simon felt strength and support fill his soul. He could not explain it. He felt a reassurance that everything would be alright. It was as if his best friend stood beside him, encouraging him.

A drastic change began in Simon. He no longer questioned who the man was. Subconsciously, Simon became concerned for Jesus. Deep down a resolve had been planted. He did not yet know it, but he had chosen to stand by Christ.

This resolution, unknown to Simon, was transferred from Simon to Jesus through the wordless exchange of a glance. Before the moment broke, Simon saw another expression in Jesus's eyes, a deep sense of gratitude.

Simon mistook the gratitude to mean an expression of thanks for carrying the cross. For walking the remaining distance to the crucifixion site. Simon knew it would be physically taxing for himself. He believed if Jesus carried the cross the rest of the way, it would kill him.

Then Simon reasoned, "A death from energy exertion would undoubtedly be more tolerable than the slow agonizing death on the cross. Maybe I am doing him an injustice by carrying the cross."

His thought immediately changed, and he considered, "Death is a portal rarely desired. He must be grateful that his life will continue a little longer, increasing the chance that some act of God will save him from this situation."

Both his conclusions about Jesus's gratitude were misinterpreted. Yes, a small portion of gratitude was directed toward Simon for carrying the cross, but the real cause behind the gratitude was for the transition Jesus had seen within Simon. At first, he had seen shock, confusion, abhorrence for the circumstances, fear for his career, and the importance of saving face. Then Jesus saw the transition of Simon's heart. Though subtle, it was a change nonetheless. Jesus knew he too had a friend by his side.

As quickly as the gaze had started, it ended. Jesus broke eye contact and looked straight ahead, down the road that led to his death.

Again, Simon registered the mocks that pierced the air, the soldiers' lashing out, the heat of the sun, and crushing weight of the wood.

Jesus positioned himself behind Simon and placed his right shoulder under the cross. He put his right hand on the main beam to help steady the cross and placed his left hand on Simon's shoulder to help stabilize himself. Jesus seemed determined to continue carrying his own burden. Simon felt some of the weight transfer off his shoulder. He was in awe of the man called Jesus.

At the crack of a whip, the two took a step forward in unison. The loud snap was close to Simon's right ear and left it ringing for the next few minutes. However, when the whip cracked, Simon felt a slight jerk on his shoulder from Jesus's hand. This was immediately followed by a small splattering on the back of Simon's head. His stomach churned as he instinctively knew what the moist spray meant.

Chapter VII

-|-

Ten Days Before
Tuesday, March 24—1:00 pm

"**S**imon, my friend. It is always a pleasure to see you," Titus exclaimed as he made his way across the busy promenade of Caesarea Maritima toward Simon. "I hope you had a pleasant crossing."

"Aside from our tempestuous departure, we did. Other than that, better weather could not have been asked for," responded Simon.

"Good, good," replied Titus.

The two men embraced as good friends do.

Titus inquired further, "How much are we unloading today?"

"None. I am simply maintaining relations, expanding our trade routes, inspecting our commercial hubs, and if possible, exploring new opportunities."

Consternation crossed Titus's face. "Has it not become your custom to bring one of your sons on such a trip?"

"I had hoped my youngest would experience his first journey. Unfortunately, an injury impeded his ability to accompany me."

"'Tis a pity," responded Titus. "I have been so impressed by your eldest, Alexander, that I anticipate meeting Rufus. Perhaps on your next voyage."

"I hope so," said Simon.

Desiring to be of some assistance, since no merchandise was to be unloaded, Titus asked, "What luggage do you have? I will get some of my men to carry it to the shop."

Titus was the most friendly, amiable person Simon knew. He could count on Titus with full confidence, which was the reason Simon considered him his right-hand man. Nevertheless, Titus was not one to do physical labor. He had a knack for delegating that Simon had never seen in anyone else. One would never be in want of assistance or service when in the presence of Titus. At the same time, such aid would never come by Titus's own hand, but always through his orders to others.

"Not necessary my friend. All I have is here in my satchel." Simon turned to his side to show the small leather bag slung over his shoulder.

"But," Simon continued, "a hearty meal with some of your wine would be a warm welcome. Having only eaten hard cakes, biscuits, and the disappointing wine of the ship during the crossing, my stomach desires to know flavorful food again."

"Right this way," Titus said as he pivoted around, and the two walked side by side.

Having arrived on one of the Herodian naval vessels, the ship had been directed to dock in the second basin of the harbor. This was in front of the provincial warehouse vaults on the south side of the temple of Augustus.

Caesarea Maritima was Simon's most important port. Gaining access in Rome's capital of the Judean province had been key to his success. Only one other merchant had the privileged access that Simon had achieved here.

The port was the busiest along the Mediterranean's eastern shore. It stood as a testament to man's will to tame nature. Without a natural harbor, it was the first port built directly in the sea. Two massive breakwaters had been constructed to thwart the ravages of the waves. The northern arm jutted out from the rocky shore, nearly due west directly into the deepening waters. The southern arm curved out, up, and straight east, looking much like a fishing hook, to meet the northern arm where the mouth of the harbor marked the safe haven within.

Six bronze statues, three on the east and three on the west side of the port's entrance towered over entering and exiting ships. On the inside of the harbor, the breakwaters were lined with warehouses to store the vast quantities of goods that came and went. Vessels of all sizes were docked in front of each warehouse. More than a hundred ships could safely be moored within the protective embrace of the harbor.

A broad promenade paralleled the warehouses, providing easy access to all the docked ships. This space also provided ample room for the rows upon rows of pots filled with valuable olive oil, spices from the east, perfumes, wines, stacks of leather, a variety of colorful stones, and marble destined for imperial mosaics ready to be shipped to every corner of the Empire.

As Simon and Titus walked into Caesarea Maritima's bustling open Forum, behind the temple of Augustus, Simon casually said, more as a statement than a question, "I presume you've managed to get all in order and operating smoothly."

Titus looked at Simon with little emotion and replied in a low voice, "Discord has increased, but let us not speak of it here where some wandering ears may hear."

Loud cheering was heard to the south, undoubtedly the joy of spectators seeing the demise of a chariot competitor or the victory of another at the hippodrome. Indeed, forty years prior, when Herod had ordered the original site renovated, expanded, and improved, he included every delight known to Rome. Renaming the city Caesarea Maritima was Herod's tribute to Caesar Augustus. In so doing, he communicated a strong message to the Emperor and to the eastern province that Rome was in Judea to stay.

Simon and Titus walked through the marketplace and onto the main thruway of the city.

Passing the first merchant office on the street, Titus said, "No change there."

"One of these days," said Simon.

It was a location Simon had tried to purchase multiple times. However, the prideful owner, a loyalist of Herod, refused to sell on the grounds that the Herodian navy required the space. This was the only port where Simon conducted business that the first merchant office from the ships was not owned by Simon. He settled for the next best option: the location directly adjacent. It was there that Titus and Simon entered.

Once inside the lobby, Simon asked, "How is discord still an issue?"

"It grows and continues to ravage our land. Once mere rumor has now grown into heated arguments. Debates divide not only Caesarea, but every developed patch of land in Judea," said Titus.

The two walked through the lobby and into Titus's office. Titus lounged on a cushion that was next to a small ornate wooden table. Atop this table sat various documents, a signing quill, and a small brass bell. Titus grabbed the bell and shook it rapidly three times. Instantly, a servant entered dressed in orient attire.

"Some wine, meat, and bread," ordered Titus.

The servant bowed and went to retrieve the food.

"You are still standing," Titus said to Simon. "Sit, sit," he offered, indicating another cushion.

As if no break in his explanation of the local discord had taken place, Titus continued in his embellished and drawn-out manner.

"Though the tide of tumult has been rising for nearly three years, the true inception of our hardships began with James. He is the lead caravan driver; you know the one I mean. Almost a year ago, he brought rumors about a man feeding an entire multitude with only a fish and a biscuit, or something of the like. I would have dismissed him immediately for spreading false rumors, but three other men also testified to the truthfulness of the story. By the voice of four men, I had no grounds for dismissal.

"Nobody believed them, of course. The lot of them are known for their often-inebriated state. But they are a hard-working crew and are dependable when it comes to travel, security, and logistics. I've heard it said, should any robbers wreak havoc upon our convoys, these four men will breathe fire upon them. Perhaps, this is why they are so commonly found with bottles. But that is neither here nor there.

"Anyway, they would not simply tell their story and leave it at that. They recounted the tale every chance they got. Their boisterous voices have incited the community to choose sides. Those who believe what they say and those who do not. If their voices were not enough, the fire of faction has been fed by additional logs of rumor.

"Little by little, travelers and merchants have brought new stories. I've even overheard imperial troops speaking of one who heals the sick and lame, cures the sight of the blind, and brings the dead back to life. Can you imagine? What absurdity! The dead back to life indeed."

Just then, the servant returned with a platter filled with cuts of dried meat, a loaf of bread, two goblets, and a small cask of wine. He set the platter on the table, filled the goblets, bowed, and exited the room.

Titus took a piece of meat, broke off a chunk of bread, and in between bites continued his explanation.

"Then about two weeks ago, Mark, the man who resides in the home next to mine—you know, the one who takes so long to say anything that your next birthday may expire before you hear a full thought expressed? Anyway, he was so convinced of these rumors, he took his lame child and went to find this healer. To my surprise, the boy returned running and bounding as if he had never spent a day off his feet.

"My curiosity was piqued. Even though I knew it would take an entire evening to get the story from him, I went to Mark's home and inquired about what had transpired. He told me the following:

"Shortly after leaving Caesarea, they heard rumors that the healer was passing through the region nearby. After a few days, he caught up to the man who was encircled by a multitude. He pushed through the throng, seeking to bring his son to the man. Several others had also brought their infants and children to be blessed by the healer. Some of the man's followers, disciples he called them, sought to keep the children back. Yet the healer, whose name he said was Jesus, chastened them telling them to let the little ones come to him. Mark was allowed to go forward, holding his son in his arms. Face to face with Jesus, Mark did not know what to say. Which does not surprise me.

"Mark said he felt as if his desires were understood and known by Jesus. Jesus outstretched his arms and Mark transferred his son from his own arms to those of Jesus. Gently holding the boy, Jesus quietly whispered in his ear. The boy, who had been quiet and shy, looked up at Jesus with a broad smile. Jesus smiled back and moved to set him on the ground. Mark said he was shocked to see Jesus did not move to set him down in a sitting manner, rather he set him so his feet touched the ground in a standing position. Mark was amazed to see his boy standing perfectly by his own strength. His legs were still lacking in muscle, but they functioned.

"Apparently, the boy walked all the way home, skipping, running, and jumping around. By the time they returned, his legs were as strong and full as any youth his same age."

Titus paused in his story as if contemplating the significance of the healing. In that small pause, Simon interjected. "How has this increased discord?"

"Ah yes," continued Titus, remembering the purpose of his

recount. "Prior to leaving, Mark was taught by some of Jesus's disciples and brought those teachings here. Over the past week, Mark has consistently testified that this Jesus is not only a healer but also the Messiah of Israel. You can imagine what ruckus such a bold statement has made. He does not allow his voice to be silenced. Every day he goes around teaching what he learned. Together, with those that witnessed the feeding of thousands, they have caused quite the division here. You of all people know there are countless religions and deities proclaimed throughout the Empire. We have seen the rising of numerous false prophets and messiahs. They gain a following and often incite their followers to riotous actions and revolts. How many radical groups have been suppressed and destroyed by the Romans?"

Simon simply nodded his head, acknowledging the fact.

"Not only do we have a division among our own nation over these rumors, but it has created alarm among the Romans. I mean, what superstitious Roman would not become uneasy if those they subjugated proclaimed they had one who could bring the dead back to life? The Empire does not take that well. We have a trifecta issue at hand; those who believe and those who don't. All the while Rome is watching, ready to decimate if needed. In passing, I've seen the fear in their eyes. No one wants to fight an army of the formerly dead."

Titus continued mournfully, "It would have been better to live in the days of Isaiah, Moses, or with our fathers Abraham, Isaac, or Jacob. Then we would know who truly spoke God's word and who to follow. Today is nothing but bickering between differing sects. All confusion with no guiding light.

"Religious disputes have riddled this town since its inception, such is the case of a city that sits on the crossroads of so many cultures, religions, and political opinions. If Rome has taught us anything, it is to pay tribute to the Emperor and abide by each other's differences. For those who recognize the advantage of such a society, opportunity abounds.

"You have taught me that more than any other person. Why, when we first met, I would not stand within three-rod lengths of a Roman."

Simon interrupted with a friendly jab. "Shocking for a man with a Roman name."

"I never knew my father, but my mother decided to honor the man who won her heart and bestowed upon me his name, even though her family and Rabbi protested her choice. Yet, to save my soul I was basically raised by the Rabbi. I knew nothing outside the gospel, which I had been taught from birth to adulthood. I grew prideful of my family and culture. My pride kept me poor and unable to accept others different than myself.

"Now look at me, I have servants from the east and am rubbing shoulders with Romans every day. In accepting others and seeing how we assist each other, I have grown, progressed, and am not bad off either. Through it all, I am now stronger in my religious convictions than ever before.

"But for the commoner, who cannot see beyond his nose, a different scenario plays out. Those we employ have divided. To put three men of differing opinions on the same task is to open the door of strife. I have done my best to keep heads cool and tempers at bay. Most days the men tolerate each other, but there have been days when I have told everyone to go home so as to avoid scuffles. It's getting worse. I will not be surprised when daggers fly."

Nodding, Simon replied, "These are troubling times. Romans brought technology, roads, aqueducts, increased commerce, and a sense of security, all of which are beneficial. Roman expansion has also mingled in new viewpoints, opinions, and religions all causing strife and confusion. People are forced to think, to question, and see if they agree with new ideas or remain true to their original beliefs. Others have given up trying to figure it all out and simply accept anything they hear. Some shut themselves off, rejecting anything different from what they learned as children. This has led many to rise up, seeking to regain their own lands, govern themselves, or establish a region controlled by their religion. To say many Jews do not desire this would be an act of ignorance. We must learn to live with others. To accept each other. To respect each other. Therein lies the way to success. And, may I be so bold as to say, between the ways of the Romans and the traditional culture of the Jews, there is space for correcting views."

Titus cut in, "You have always been a radical thinker, my friend."

Simon defended Titus's underlying accusation. "Worry not, I know who my God is. I desire to serve him faithfully and eagerly await the Savior who will free us. But, in the meantime, I find it safest to respect the world around us. Therein we gain from the prosperity it offers. I seek to learn the best values that are different from my own and apply them to my life. I live according to my convictions and do not let the opinions of the world thwart my faith."

With a smile, he added, "After all, the better I know others, the more wealth I can make from them."

Turning the conversation from its philosophical course back to the matter at hand, Simon said, "I have heard of this Jesus. Though I have traveled in this region numerous times, I have never seen him. Stories of his miracles have reached Cyrene. After all, I was the one who took half of them there. Perhaps the distance from Jerusalem to Cyrene has saved us from the turmoil found here. We have largely dismissed the stories as nothing more than tales from Judea. No one has any ties to the miracles; thus, they are seen only as rumors and stories. Here, where people have seen and have been healed by this Jesus, I can see where confusion would arise. Those whose lives have been touched by him cannot deny him. Yet, those who have no connection to him are reluctant to accept him. How many follow this Jesus?" asked Simon.

"Here? Few, but they are boisterous and determined in their convictions."

"What are their convictions?"

"Some say this Jesus is a great prophet, while others proclaim him as the Son of God."

"Interesting. Even they have discord among themselves. Do you allow them to work together, or have you separated them?"

"I have tried both. At first, I kept them working together. Yet, so many arguments arose that I began separating them. However, this disjointed the teams and process."

"And now daggers may fly."

"Daggers will fly regardless. In any other profession, I could simply dismiss them. However, if I remove any individual group, it may weaken or break contacts tied to those groups. If this following of Jesus increases, it would be advantageous to maintain good relationships with those who follow him."

Simon chuckled. "Titus, you are starting to sound like me. Seven years ago, you would never have thought that way. I agree though. Loyalty with our contacts lies heavily with you. This central port puts you in communication with them far more frequently than I. You must do what is best to ensure future relations. I trust your judgment. You are wise in your dealings with men and have never let me down."

Titus smiled and retorted, "I am a mere link in the chain when it comes to retaining loyalties. As my men here are to me, I am to you. You are the anchor upon which the chain is hung."

Chapter VIII

-|-

Day Of
Friday, April 3—8:10 am

He felt their hate. He saw it in their eyes. They kept their distance, appearing distinguished, penitent, and devoted to religion. Their glances toward Jesus betrayed a masked humility and revealed their satisfaction in his demise. Their eyes portrayed a sense of victory and desire to see this man destroyed.

The crowd fed off the hate that emanated from these distinguished ones. Their minions were sent to do that which their masters would not do. They followed close to the procession like pesky flies, buzzing and humming in constant motion. They would venture close enough to let spit fly or fling another taunt. When one was pushed back, another moved in.

Frustration showed on the faces of the soldiers as they constantly had to wedge their way through the crowd. Simon could not tell which they detested more, having to accompany Jesus to the place of his crucifixion or the pressing irksome crowd. The soldiers lashed out at Jesus, as much as at the annoying vermin that impeded forward progression.

Aside from the trailing distinguished leaders and pressing commoners, there was another group Simon noticed. These were silent in terms of comments but audible by way of weeping. Their faces streamed with tears. Their features were taut with anxiety. Their eyes were windows to their breaking hearts. They did not want to behold Jesus in his beaten condition, nor hear the incessant jeers being yelled at him; neither did they want this procession of crucifixion to be real. Nevertheless, love for Jesus brought their eyes back to him time and time again. Each glance broke their hearts a little more.

They saw his bruises and cuts. His blood-soaked clothing attested to the flogging his back had sustained. His labored stride testified to the strain and exhaustion encompassing his physical frame. They saw the wreath of thorns crowning his head, mocking what the multitude continually challenged. Lastly, they saw the means of his death, carried by Jesus and a stranger they did not know. They knew with each step, Jesus was closer to his final moment.

It was not hard to deduce these were Jesus's friends and family. Simon could only imagine what it must be like to watch your own son, brother, or friend be brutally beaten and crucified. The concern and pain Simon felt for his children when they were sick or injured was but a drop compared to the torment that must be felt by someone witnessing the forced death of a loved one.

Simon had never known someone who had been crucified. Crucifixion was nothing new in the Empire. Only the blind would have never witnessed one, but even without sight, they were aware of what it entailed. It was common to have crosses erected on the main roads leading into and out of a city. Crosses were occupied by the worst of criminals, whose cries of anguish and affliction bleated in the ears of passersby. Romans saved this slow tormenting form of capital punishment for those deemed a threat to the Empire such as traitors, radicals, and revolutionaries. The method stood as a warning to all who opposed Caesar, in an effort to instill obedience and establish dominance over the populace.

Jesus was definitely strong enough to pose a threat to Rome, or at least had been prior to his beating and flogging. Anyone who could withstand such treatment and carry a cross at all would have to be a man of great strength. Be that as it may, Simon could not envision Jesus being the kind who would fight against Rome. He saw him as one who would be a great citizen of the Empire.

Simon's ponderings ceased, the physical labor of carrying the cross demanded his full attention. Simon, who had no injuries, a full night's sleep, and some small but hearty cakes for breakfast was struggling with the weight and awkwardness of the cross. He had never regarded himself as one of great stature, but he did consider himself one with great endurance. Nevertheless, Simon's physical strength was waning. Each step was a determined effort. He could not operate his body in one cohesive motion. For an instant, his cognitive focus was on his shoulder and hands, in the act of balancing and carrying the cross. The next moment, he was keenly aware of each stone in the road and where to strategically place each step. Then he was distracted by the burning in his legs, throbbing muscles, and the exhaustion in his body. When he focused on these individual aspects, the ones not at the forefront of his mind deteriorated. The cross became less balanced. His feet shuffled and caught on the uneven surface of the street. His muscles slouched and strained.

Tipping ever so slightly to the right, Simon adjusted his hands to keep the cross from rolling off his shoulder. The effort occupied all of his mental capacity. At that moment, his toe caught on an uneven stone.

Attempting to maintain his balance, Simon gripped the cross beam with all his might, hoping the wood would act as a balancing weight. What counterweight the cross may have posed was negated by Jesus, whose own balance was thwarted by the jarring tug of Simon's trip. Once the downward fall was initiated, there was no stopping it.

Impact with the ground took only a second. Within that fraction of time, Simon felt as if hours elapsed. He felt an intense desire to protect Jesus from further injury, which caused him to instinctively maintain a firm grip on the beam and twist vigorously to his right, pulling the cross out of Jesus's hands. The twist threw the cross down upon the ground and spun Simon in the air. He landed hard on his back across the main beam of the cross.

A sharp pain shot through his body. Dust swirled around him. He closed his eyes wondering if his back had broken. Immediately, his eyes shot open when he remembered Jesus.

Simon rolled off the cross, turned, and sought to know if Jesus had been spared from the fall. A sliver of relief came over him as he caught a glimpse of Jesus who had not fallen on the cross, nor had any section of the cross fallen on him. However, deep remorse filled Simon as he saw Jesus sprawled face down on the ground. Simon had been the one to cause this accident. Jesus had been through enough torture and the worst was yet to come. For Simon, the thought of having caused him more bruises and cuts was unbearable.

This was a concern Simon had not considered, until this moment but once this idea took center stage, it enveloped his being. He would save Jesus from additional wounds if he could. He would shield him from the wrath of the soldiers and crowd. He would carry the cross alone.

Simon quickly crawled the few inches to Jesus and helped turn him on his side. He saw excruciating pain in Jesus's facial and body expressions. All the beatings and lashings had not numbed his senses. Jesus curled into the fetal position. A gurgle and wince from his throat accompanied by a slight muscular twitching of his arms and legs testified to his great agony. Simon was not sure if the twitching was caused by the fall or from an inner struggle to keep from crying out and weeping. Jesus's left hand was pressed against the side of his head. No doubt in an effort to ease the pain in his skull, having impacted the hard stone pavement. For the first time, Simon took distinct notice of the crown of thorns that had been placed on Jesus's head. No doubt when Jesus's head hit the ground, thorns were pushed deeper into his skin.

Tears fell from Simon's eyes. He had been the cause of additional wounds. Had he been more diligent in placing his feet, they would not have fallen. There was nothing he could do to ease Jesus's pain. He noticed people laughing and the legionaries ready to use force to get Jesus and Simon back on their feet.

Kneeling over Jesus, Simon held his hands over him to protect him. He glanced up at the soldiers and cried out, "Let him be."

Taken back by the savage plea, they stayed their feet and hands, which were poised to strike.

Gently, Simon took Jesus by the shoulders and pulled him to a sitting position. Simon got to his own feet, reached out, clasped Jesus's hands, and pulled him to his feet. Simon knew helping Jesus stand would save him from the kicks and lashes that would inevitably come from the impatient soldiers.

With Jesus standing directly in front of him, Simon could not bring himself to look him in the eye. Shameful sorrow filled his soul for having tripped.

Keeping his head bowed, he quietly said, "I am sorry to have caused you more pain."

Another tear rolled down his cheek. In an effort to mask his internal torment, Simon quickly turned, bent down, and lifted the heavy cross onto his right shoulder. He was determined to carry the cross himself, saving Jesus from having to bear its burden any further.

Once on his shoulder, Simon heaved the cross up and back a few inches, to adjust the weight distribution. It pressed heavily into his shoulder, the rough wood tearing at his cloak.

As Simon was about to continue, Jesus laboriously ducked under the cross and stepped forward, so he was next to Simon with the cross between them. Jesus did not place his shoulder under the cross as before, rather, he simply stood next to Simon, raised his hand, and set it on the side of the crossbeams to help steady it. Perhaps this was done out of concern for falling again, the realization that he could not physically bear the weight of the cross, or as Simon believed, Jesus understood the torment inside Simon and was willing to allow him the inner comfort of carrying the cross alone. In so doing, Jesus conveyed to Simon his acceptance of Simon's apology and allowed Simon to cope with his internal pain. At the same time, Jesus's hand on the cross comforted Simon by letting him know that the cross was not Simon's.

Chapter IX

-|-

Thirty Days Before
Wednesday, March 4—11:00 am

The rocking of a boat never caused Simon grief. Seasickness never plagued him as it did other passengers. He welcomed the movements of the boat. Whether it was rocking bow to stern, port to starboard, or the diagonal combination of the two, he found the motion soothing.

Something about the rise and fall of the boat reminded him of his youth. Those days when the stresses of life did not weigh upon his mind. When life was spent playing in the fields and hills near his home. When the travails of life had not taught him of the difficulties and cruelness of the world. Younger years when his only concern was to drink when thirsty, eat when hungry, and sleep when his energy was spent. All the decisions and challenges of life were taken care of by his parents and leaders. Those days remained fond in his memory and for some reason, the sea brought those youthful years to the forefront of his thoughts.

Simon leaned against the railing of the naval ship. The gentle wind filled the sails and steadily propelled the ship forward. The fragrance of the sea, the squawking of sea birds, the crashing of the bow through the waves, and the roll of the ship brought a smile to his face.

He leaned over the rail and watched the water glide past the side of the ship. He was struck with awe at the ability of such a heavy vessel to float and to cut so effortlessly through the water.

Land was no longer in sight. The deep blue sea spread out in all directions as far as the eye could see. Aside from the horizon to the northwest, which was dominated by heavy dark clouds, in all other directions the sea and sky seemed to become one. Differentiating where water ended and air began was a challenge.

He watched the waves and let himself be transfixed by their continuous motion. For a moment, his mind went blank; all that remained was the sensation of the rise and fall of the ship. He observed the dancing light in the water, shimmering refracted veins that blended, separated, and intertwined on the water's surface. He traced the bands down into the expanse of the sea where the water's shade darkened to a foreboding abyss, a depth Simon did not comprehend. How deep did it go? What swam or lay at the bottom? Did creatures look up and see a bright horizon or were their eyes unable to perceive the space beyond the water's surface, thus, the hull of a boat being an oddity that penetrated their world from a realm they couldn't understand?

From the moment the ship sailed, Simon stood near the stern, watching the shoreline until it vanished from sight. Each time he saw his homeland slip below the horizon, his sense of adventure increased. His excitement ignited further, days later, when a different land appeared off the bow of the ship. Even though he had crossed the sea multiple times, the exhilarating sensation of seeing land disappear and reappear never dissipated.

One additional detail made his enjoyment of crossing the sea satisfying. This was experiencing it with his son and seeing amazement in his eyes.

Two years prior, for the first time, Simon brought his eldest son Alexander on one of his journeys. Alexander melted in despair when the coast of their homeland fell out of view and Simon spent the following days reassuring him that his mother, brother, friends, and their home were still safe and eagerly awaiting their return. When the coast of Judea came into view, Alexander had jumped about on deck, shouting and hollering for joy that they would soon be home.

Utter bewilderment crossed Alexander's face when the breakwaters and bronze statues of Caesarea Maritima became distinguishable.

"What is the matter?" Simon had inquired.

"This is not our home," responded Alexander in a confused tone.

Though Simon had told Alexander about foreign cities and regions, Alexander had not fully comprehended their significance. That day, as Simon introduced his eldest boy to Titus on the docks, Alexander began to understand. The seed was planted. From that day forward, Alexander constantly wanted to join Simon on his travels. The same amazement Simon felt in discovering something new had become visible in the eyes of his son.

Simon and Alexander often talk about that voyage. It continued to be a fond experience that brought the two closer together.

As he stood next to the ship's railing and recalled that wonderful experience, his happiness ebbed as he thought about how much he wished his second son, Rufus, had come on this voyage. Simon would have loved to see how he reacted to his first sea crossing. Would he be as concerned as Alexander had been? Would he find it as exhilarating as Simon did? Would he and Rufus build a strong relationship as he had with Alexander?

Hopefully, these questions would be answered the next time Simon went to Jerusalem.

"Simon," said a commanding voice behind him.

Simon turned to see the captain of the ship.

"I'm informed you desire to help with duties on the ship."

"As always," replied Simon.

"Ah, yes. On one of these voyages, I keep hoping you will be content to simply enjoy the ride."

"As much as I love the waves, I can only watch them for so long before I start feeling like my life is wasting away, and I cannot stay in my cabin without getting antsy," said Simon.

"Very well. Though this vessel is as loyal as the God Neptune, a few of her seams are in need of internal repair. Go below and find Celsus. He will not be hard to find, since he is the only one that must hunch below decks. He will inform you of your duties."

The captain smiled and smacked Simon on the shoulder. "Always a pleasure to have you aboard. If all Jews were as accepting as you, what an Empire we would have!"

Simon could not help but give a friendly jab in response. "If all Romans were as amiable as you, what would Rome do with all their legions?"

"Quite right, my friend, quite right."

The captain turned and continued his inspection of the ship. Simon looked at the waves once more, before descending into the depths of the vessel.

Chapter X

-|-

Day Of
Friday, April 3—8:15 am

Simon's steps had become mechanical. No longer did he waver between foot and hand. He had the clear conscience of knowing if he fell, he would not make Jesus fall as well. His body bore the weight of the cross and his muscles moved him forward.

His mind had numbed to his surroundings. Observations of the people around him had ceased. He was either disgusted by their actions or could not bear to see their broken hearts. No longer did he hear their shouts and taunts. Nor did he care about their words. He knew they were wrong.

The man who walked by his side, still helping to balance the cross, was not the devil. No devil could express love through a mere glance. He was not a deceiver. No deceiver would take such a brutal beating without confessing their fault in hope of avoiding death. Since he was not a deceiver, he could be no liar. For deceivers and liars seek their own gain. When their plan goes awry, they change their deception to improve their circumstances.

Simon had seen liars punished before. As they were dragged away for punishment, they pleaded for forgiveness and promised to correct their ways or sought to place blame on an outside source.

If those pleas did not improve their situation, they digressed to spewing insults and threats. In essence, they said anything that might sway the minds of their punishers.

In contrast to such scheming humans, Jesus did not plead to be forgiven. He did not say he would correct his ways. He did not mock the people. He did not curse them. In fact, he only spoke once. This was when they paused momentarily, while the soldiers made way for them to proceed through the west gate. A group of grieving women was standing near Jesus. He asked them not to weep for him, but rather for themselves, their children, and Israel, because of the suffering that would come upon them.

One of the religious leaders heard this and declared it a curse toward Israel, which caused the mob to spew forth their hate more robustly.

Simon was confused by what Jesus had said. He did not know what it meant. The tone in Jesus's voice did not hold an edge of revenge or desire to see Israel punished. Thus, Simon believed his words were not a curse or threat. Rather, the tone seemed sorrowful, as if predicting or prophesying what might come. His message was not only for those he loved but also for those who even now cursed him. Simon instinctively knew Jesus's concern for others did not end with those currently around him. Indeed, what he had said applied to all of Israel.

The few words Jesus spoke were not as thought-provoking as the two most commonly shouted phrases from the crowd. These were challenges to Jesus's character and identity, both of which caused Simon to ponder their significance.

"How odd," considered Simon, "that they challenge Jesus to save himself."

Because of his beaten condition, Simon struggled to believe Jesus could free himself from the situation. Though Jesus was walking by his own strength, the physical activity of doing so was requiring all his energy. Not for an instant did Simon believe Jesus could run or fight his way to freedom. The soldiers would stop him before he took two steps. Should, by some miracle, Jesus get past them, the mass of people was so packed together, they created a barrier as formidable as the wall that encircled the city.

"No," speculated Simon, "there is no way he can save himself."

At the moment of this deduction, he felt a strange calm come over his whole being. Never had he experienced such tranquility before. The feeling brought with it a piece of knowledge. He could not explain it, yet somehow, he believed if this man wanted to be saved from his torment, indeed Jesus could somehow bring it to pass. Simon thought it laughable. Only an act of God could keep this man from death. Yet the feeling persisted. He strongly felt that no one had power over Jesus.

Struggling to understand this feeling, Simon considered the second challenge so boisterously expressed. He thought this one to be more radical, that of Jesus being the Messiah.

"If this man is the Messiah, there is no doubt he can save himself by calling upon the hosts of heaven. Though, if he is the Messiah, why would he not call upon his heavenly army to aid him? Angels," Simon envisioned, "would swoop in and take him from this place and reap swift punishment on all involved with his sentence. On the other hand, if he is Israel's deliverer, why would he be in such a horrible situation? Should not all Israelites be eager to follow him? Would they not sally forth under his leadership to free themselves from their oppressors and again establish the kingdom of God on Earth?"

Simon did not know what to think of this Messianic challenge. He could not say if Jesus was or was not the Messiah. If he was, Simon was disappointed to think that Jesus had failed in his destined calling. How else would the Messiah end up in such a situation? All he knew was Jesus did not appear like the savior he had imagined. He had always pictured a more robust, militant type, with eyes of flames, wielding a powerful sword, uniting all Israel, and governing them in justice. Simon had never regarded him to be a common man, with eyes of compassion and love, carrying a wooden cross.

Clarification, much like a blanket for the soul, filled Simon. The same peace he had felt moments before again pierced his heart and mind. It was as if an unseen messenger was whispering knowledge to him, that Jesus was a man of God, that he was innocent, that he had the power to free himself, and that he was the long-prophesied Savior.

It was more than Simon could understand. He did not comprehend it. All his reasoning seemed to negate the sensation that burned within him. Nevertheless, when all was said and done, the feeling of assurance remained.

— — —

Originally, Simon could have made a case for the injustice of being compelled to carry the cross. But after the stumble, helping Jesus to stand, and his determination to carry the whole weight of the cross, he had become fully involved. All of these acts testified that he had accepted the task. Though originally an innocent bystander, he had chosen sides. He did not understand how, but he had learned for himself the character and identity of Jesus. Simon stood with him and opposed those who sought his death.

After a few more steps, Simon took note of the blood that covered his clothing. He was not sure if it was Jesus's or his own. It was almost entirely on his right side, except for some streaks on his left sleeve and chest. These splotches came from Jesus, caused when Simon assisted him to his feet. On his right side, the blood had come from the cross. All the jostling caused it to transfer from the cross onto Simon's cloak. Perspiration had soaked through the undergarments on his back and chest. The sweat merged with the blood, causing it to slowly streak down his garments. It made it appear as if Simon had sustained a nasty gash on his shoulder, which could very well be the case. The coarse wood constantly dug into his shoulder. With each step, it scraped his cloak and wore his flesh raw.

At one point, Simon noticed a drop of blood that had run from the cross to his hand. He felt it slowly bead up and run down his forearm. When it reached his elbow, it wobbled back and forth with the motion of his body. Eventually, it fell away, missing the hem of his sagging sleeve and landing on the dusty road.

The sight tormented him. It testified to his own pain and the pain of the man walking by his side.

Though Jesus kept his hand on the cross, it had stopped acting as a stabilizing force. Rather, the cross acted as a balance for Jesus. Simon felt the increasing weight of Jesus as he used the beam more and more to stabilize himself, and Simon became warier of his own footing, afraid of losing his balance again.

After exiting the city gate, the street widened. With more walking space, progression continued uninhibited. Unfortunately, Jesus's energy was waning. His walk resembled a shuffle rather than a stride and, as a result, Simon was forced to slow his own pace. The thought of letting Jesus fall behind filled Simon with horror. Doing so would leave Jesus to the soldiers. In hopes of saving Jesus from the whips that would inevitably fall upon his back, Simon feigned an even more exhausted countenance than that of Jesus. He slowed his walk, slouched more, groaned and winced at the awkwardness of the cross, and began to heave for breath. This was not an entire act. He was indeed tired and exhausted. He simply made it more obvious that he was struggling.

"Better to let them think I am the one tiring," Simon decided. "That should bring their wrath on me, rather than him."

From time to time, Simon glanced over the beam to Jesus. His eyes looked numb and in a distressful daze. He found it surprising that Jesus was still conscious.

"How does he manage to keep going? His pain must be extremely acute, combined with the amount of blood he has lost; it is a marvel he is even standing."

At that moment, Simon's body told him something had changed in the contour of the road.

Ever so slightly, the path they were on began to incline. Immediately, Simon felt the added strain of the upward slope. His eyes focused and were filled with dread. Ahead loomed Golgotha.

From this point on their route was uphill. It was not a steep hill, nor a long hill, but it was a rise. Simon wondered if his legs could continue. Would his strength give out? The cross instantly felt heavier. His energy plummeted. It was too much to bear. He could not go another step. All he had to do was throw the cross down and declare he could go no farther. Surely, the centurion seeing his fatigued condition would order someone else to take his place.

His stride decreased with each step. The weight of the cross bore down on his shoulder like a massive boulder. He no longer had to feign increased fatigue. He felt as if his energy was completely depleted with no reserve to draw upon.

His conscience told him he did not deserve such treatment. He had nothing to do with the sentencing of Jesus. This idea broke to the forefront of his mind so quickly that Simon accepted it before he realized what he was thinking.

Fifteen minutes had elapsed from the time he had been compelled to carry the cross. To Simon, it seemed like an eternity. Initially, he had been adamant about not getting involved. He had work to complete and relationships to cultivate. He had been compelled into this service but having given a solid effort, he reasoned he was justified in abandoning the task. Did not his exhaustion give him the right to pass the burden to someone else? Perhaps to one of the bystanders who were eager for the crucifixion to take place. Surely, they would reject the responsibility on the same grounds Simon had, but as he had been, so too could they be compelled.

These justifying thoughts were unrelenting, endeavoring to convince Simon to give up. They created every excuse possible to sway his actions in their favor. It was almost as if an unseen being was trying to dissuade him from carrying the cross. As if trying to stop the crucifixion.

"Throw the cross down."

"Run away."

"Stop moving."

"If you step to the right, you can make him fall."

"Push the cross onto Jesus."

"Do you think you can make him bleed more?"

"The messiah cannot bleed; this is an imposter."

These dark temptations blared in Simon's mind. He shook his head to put them away, but they continued relentlessly. His physical battle of carrying the cross had been flanked by his own mind. His body was screaming for rest, his brain clamoring to desist from the unjust punishment he had received. Darkness reached into his being, discouraging him from helping Jesus and also persuading him to stop the crucifixion. The peace that had calmed and enlightened his soul moments before, was nowhere to be found.

At this moment of inner turmoil, Simon felt a slight movement. Among all the commotion around him and his physical exhaustion, he was surprised he even noticed it.

Jesus's hand slowly moved from the cross to Simon's upper arm and something about his touch gave Simon strength.

Was it strength? After all, his body was exhausted, his muscles fatigued, his shoulder throbbing, his arms numb. Nevertheless, Simon felt a rising determination to go on. Energy beyond his own gave him the force to endure the physical pain. The commotion in his mind ceased. He remembered his resolve, the one he had made a few minutes before, to stand with Jesus. He wondered how he had forgotten it so quickly.

Though these changes were necessary for Simon to continue, there was one thing that made his determination ironclad. It was a reversal of the role Simon thought he held. From the beginning, Simon was sure he was helping Jesus. Now, it seemed more accurate that Jesus was helping him. Simon felt no matter how much he defended and aided Jesus, Jesus would always provide more support.

Simon awkwardly turned his head to look at Jesus, who was staring straight back. Jesus nodded his head. Sheer understanding was in his eyes. Simon knew he did not have to explain his condition. Jesus knew his pain, fatigue, how far he could go, and how much energy and determination was needed to finish the task.

"How can he understand me so well?" mused Simon. "After years spent with my wife, I have never seen the level of understanding in her eyes that I see in his."

Had it not been for the kindness, compassion, and trust Simon saw in his eyes, he would have considered Jesus an odd phenomenon. The kind of person he would protect his family against. The kind whose words speak one thing, but their eyes and intentions say another. The kind of person who cannot be trusted.

This was not the case with Jesus. His stare could be intimidating, yet at the same time filled with peace and understanding. His physical stature did not command respect, but his presence did. His appearance would not draw attention favorably or negatively, yet his presence conveyed trust and friendship. His movements would not generate praise or scoffs, but his composure was calm and under complete control. His voice was not majestic or weak, but it was powerful.

For the first time, Simon really took note of Jesus's features, striving to see him without his wounds. He was a young man, probably in his early thirties. His features were strong, but not bulky. His face was familiar. His presence, welcoming. Kindness, concern, love, and understanding emanated from his being. Simon had seen all of those attributes in the eyes of others, but never all at the same time.

Jesus puzzled Simon. He did not comprehend how Jesus could be so loving and understanding, especially in the very moment he was being treated so horribly. Simon did not know how Jesus could give strength despite being so exhausted, and Simon did not understand why Jesus seemed to care so much for a complete stranger.

Contempt, hatred, and disgust never crossed the face of Jesus. In fact, Simon saw the same compassion and concern toward the crowd and soldiers, as he saw directed at himself.

"This is no ordinary man," concluded Simon.

That definitive piece of knowledge stuck. No other ideas ebbed their way in to take its place. Simon's mind cleared. All questions disappeared. His concerns fled. All that remained was the weight of that wisdom: "He is no ordinary man."

So distracted was Simon by this thought that he did not notice they had arrived at Golgotha.

Chapter XI

-|-

Thirty Days Before
Wednesday, March 4—6:00 am

$\mathbf{F}$or now, the clouds were not threatening. They were simply there, hovering in the distance on the horizon, yet their presence could swiftly gather force with the Mediterranean feeding them.

Simon hoped the clouds would blow over. Though he enjoyed crossing the Mediterranean, he did not enjoy the adrenaline that filled his body when the sea became tempestuous. He hoped for a calm crossing.

Currently, Simon stood on a vacant section of the Apollonia dock. He watched small waves rise and fall against the stones that delineated the world of water from that of land. Being on the south side of the Mediterranean, the protected harbor never had a high or low tide, which meant ships could come and go at any time. The port was a safe haven even during the most raging storms.

Apollonia's wharf was protected from the damaging waves of violent tempests thanks to the manner of its position and structure. The port was separated into two sections: an east side, which was the main entrance, and a west side that sat within the defensive walls of the city. A canal between the two provided access one to the other. The mouth of the harbor was flanked by two man-made peninsulas or rubble breakers. On the north end, there were two small islands. Sea walls had been built to connect the islands and then arc toward the town of Apollonia. This effectively blocked the west side from the ravages of the open sea.

Apollonia, situated on the southern Mediterranean coast, was nearly due south across the waters from Athens, Greece. It was the Roman capital of the southern province of Cyrenaica. Graced by the grandeur of Rome, it was fortified by protective walls and boasted the best harbor, theater, basilicas, and an official palace in all of Libya. Thanks to the influence of the colonizing Greeks, followed by control of the Romans, Apollonia had become an important and busy coastal city. As such it was known for its spacious warehouses, ship-building facilities, and Roman naval presence. It was a main point of trade into and out of Afri-terra. A perfect hub for Simon's bustling endeavors.

Ports, such as Ostia, Alexandria, or Athens were much larger and far more competitive. Most said that to succeed in trade you had to be based in one of these major locations. Though Apollonia was on the smaller side of the port spectrum, it was the hub of Simon's business. Despite the smaller location, Simon had managed to build a wide network of influential relations and employ some of the most capable hands in the industry. In so doing, he had gained a presence in the big ports and was expanding his influence.

His dream was to be recognized as the most successful tradesman in the Empire. His days, nights, and thoughts were consumed with his business. This distanced him from his family, simply by the fact he traveled all over maintaining relationships, creating contracts, and expanding the services his company provided.

Apollonia was big enough that Simon's roots were respected, yet small enough that people were impressed with the growth he had accomplished. Other merchants held Simon in high esteem for having built such a vast trade, based as they said, "from a minor port." Many viewed him as an example of how to create and expand a business.

The admiration of men delighted Simon but what kept him up at night, what mattered most to him, was his legacy. He was determined to be remembered as the greatest businessman. He would be the leader of an empire as big as that of the Romans. He would not have legions of soldiers, but workers. He would not have centurions, but managers. He would not have a navy that established dominance of the sea, but his ships would dominate in transporting desired goods to every corner of the Empire. His name would go down in history as the one who conquered business and provided the best goods.

Simon was determined his influence would continue after his death. His legacy and accomplishments would live on through his sons.

All morning he had been occupied with the details of his approaching trip to Jerusalem. This journey was the next big step in his conquest. He was on his way to complete vital contracts that would usher in a whole new chapter of success. He could not wait for those moments when he knew wealth was being signed into existence.

For now, he needed to wait. The ship he was to board was in the final stages of preparation for departure. He stood on the stones next to the dock and watched. Supplies were manually carried onto the deck or hoisted and lowered into the ship. Cords and canvas were checked. The activity on and around the ship was as lively as an anthill.

While watching the sailors, Simon's eyes tracked along the length of the ship he would soon board. When his gaze reached the bow, it continued across the water of the harbor, over the protecting wall, and out to the majestic sky. As he scanned the horizon, his mind wandered back to the memory created the day before on the outskirts of his hometown of Cyrene.

— — —

Walking side by side in the dusk, before the rising of the sun, Simon and his wife Julia reached the outskirts of Cyrene. Ahead, the north city road descended from the plateau, upon which Cyrene was built, to the broad flatland below. The road cut across the terrace, before dropping down to the coast and on to Apollonia.

Julia always accompanied her husband to where the road made its first descent. From there she watched as he completed the first zigzag until he was out of sight. She loved him dearly. He was her best friend. Being separated from him for months on end meant months of worry and loneliness. Of course, she had their two boys to keep her company, along with friends and family. These soothed the emptiness she felt in his absence, yet none of them completed her days as he did. As much as she hated for him to leave, the precious moments spent walking together gave her reassurance and strength.

Reaching the point where Simon would continue on his own, Julia said in a quiet, yet concerned voice, "I cannot shake the feeling that your journey will be life-changing."

"My dear," Simon said with a gentle squeeze to her hand, "I assure you I will be fine."

"It's a strange feeling. I don't feel you are in danger or shouldn't go. It's not like the feeling I had three years ago. I don't know if this feeling is a good omen or a feeling of caution. I know that when you return, things will be different."

Simon had no feeling of foreboding change. To him, the voyage felt like all the others but he recognized he was not in tune with feelings like Julia. She had a gift he did not possess.

When they had first been married, he considered many of her feelings simply those of a woman, all emotion and no logic, over-concerned and over-thinking. With time he learned to trust her. Doing so had proved advantageous time and time again. She had an accurate sense of foreknowledge, not only for their family but for his work ventures. This helped them prepare for troubled times, avoid dangerous situations, and ward off those who just wanted their riches. Couple Julia's talent with Simon's intuition for business and there was no way their family could not prosper.

Simon took both her hands in his. She was his definition of beauty. Their eyes locked.

With complete conviction, he said, "Beloved, I shall return. Whatever change may come, I will strive to make the best of it."

"Be safe and be wise," Julia implored.

Her words did not represent a particular emotion, rather a conglomerate of feelings. It was said out of sorrow for his leaving, concern for his well-being, anticipation for his return, embodiment of her love, and desire that he never leave her side.

Simon smiled and said, "Your love keeps me well and safe."

Wrapping her in his arms, he bowed his head and whispered in her ear, "You are the love of my life and the rock of our family. I will miss you and I look forward to being with you again."

He gently kissed her cheeks. Then, with all the love of his heart, he kissed her lips.

Julia held the kiss and embrace.

Simon was the one to pull away and as he did, tears rolled from Julia's eyes. He gently wiped them away.

"Everything will be alright," he said reassuringly.

She silently nodded in agreement.

Turning, Simon started his journey by himself. Halfway down the first zigzag, he looked back. Just then the sun peeked over the horizon. Julia was lit in a radiant beam of yellow light. Oh, how he missed her already. He raised his hand and waved goodbye. She raised her hand, but instead of waving goodbye, pressed her fingers to her lips then lowered her hand toward Simon.

Simon turned and continued. After a minute, he went around the first corner and out of Julia's sight. Before doing so, he glanced back, pressed his fingers to his lips, and lowered his hand toward Julia.

He was too distant to make out her features but he was sure her face had broken into a broad smile.

Chapter XII

Day Of
Friday, April 3—8:20 am

"**B**le ..."

The full word did not leave his mouth. Immediately, he began again, quietly stammering, "Ble ... ssed art th ... ou."

A short pause ensued before he continued, as if gathering internal strength to speak clearly. What he said next shocked Simon to his core.

"Simon of Cyrene."

"How can he possibly know my name?" wondered Simon.

Jesus offered one more, almost inaudible sentence. "For thou hast helped me in a time of need."

Tears filled Simon's eyes. He gave no response. He was in shock that Jesus had called him by name and he did not know how to react. He was humbled by the kindness and gratitude he received from Jesus. Even if words had come, Simon would not have had the chance to utter them. No sooner had Jesus finished the phrase than he was pushed forward by one of the soldiers. Two others took the cross from Simon and threw it on the ground and Simon was shoved away like a filthy dog.

Unlike when he had first entered Jerusalem and walked

shoulder to shoulder with those around him, now people parted to avoid him. No one wanted to stand next to him. No one wanted to even brush against his clothing. To the crowd, Simon had become unclean.

Having reached Golgotha, most who had followed the procession sat on the ground to watch. Some, like Simon, remained standing. The scene was beyond what Simon wished to observe, nevertheless he could not bring himself to look away.

While the centurion and one other soldier guarded Jesus, the other eight broke into two groups of four. The two thieves had carried their own crossbeams; a much lighter weight than the full cross Jesus had brought to Golgotha. Two soldiers restrained each man, while two others lashed the men's arms to their respective crossbeam. Then the four legionaries raised the crossbeam and placed it in the notch of the permanent vertical beams. Once in place, they restrained the legs of the men, who were kicking in an effort to free themselves, and tied them to the wood as well.

The soldiers were experts at this work. Their seasoned crucifying skills, perfected from the countless times they had performed these duties, were executed without delay. The condemned were fixed in a matter of minutes, despite their attempts to break free or thwart the soldiers' efforts.

Once the two criminals were crucified, the soldiers prepared for the third and final crucifixion of the day. Two removed Jesus's cloak and threw it on the ground. The blood-soaked cloth did not faze them in the least. They instructed him to remove his undergarments and sandals. Jesus did so slowly; not to prolong the inevitable, but because the motions required to do so were difficult. Once removed, one of the soldiers used the tip of his spear to swat the items from Jesus's hands to the ground next to the cloak.

Completely naked, the full extent of the beating Jesus had sustained was visible. The bruises, cuts, and welts Simon had seen on his face and hands were dwarfed by the brutality his body, arms, and legs had sustained. His back and sides were shredded, evidence of a brutal flogging. His arms and legs had not escaped such a flesh-shattering punishment. Those who wept for Jesus turned their heads in horror. Upon seeing the mutilated body of Jesus, even those who wished his death shuddered for a split second. Simon could not watch anymore.

With his back turned on the scene, he walked to the other side of the road. His emotions were frazzled. He did not know exactly what he felt. An emptiness? He was a husk of his normal self. It was as if his soul had been stripped and left bare. His eyes looked forward yet focused on nothing. He was dazed. In shock. Numb.

Had it been a normal day, it would have been a splendid one. He would have relished the sensations of the warm sun and the light breeze. He would have found simple delight in the color of desert flowers. He would have happily greeted his friends and eagerly inquired about their lives. He would have savored the bitter taste of festival food. He would have sought solace in a lonely corner of the temple, away from the merchants and sacrifices, where he could feel a closeness to God. He felt none of the joy anticipated when he had awoken this morning. His life had become one he did not recognize.

All of a sudden, he heard a dull thud. Then another and another. The sound was rhythmic and labored. The sound of the pounding nail felt like a punch to Simon's heart. The first sounded soft, as if muffled. The ones that followed sounded hard and forced. His head bowed and tears fell from his eyes. In his blurred vision, he saw his own hands. They were cut and bleeding from splinters that were wedged in the skin of his palms.

"I didn't help him," he thought. "I carried his cross, hastening his crucifixion. Perhaps there was something I could have done to stop it, but instead, I submitted and assisted in bringing him to this awful place. I am no better than the soldiers or this angry crowd."

More tears fell and his shoulders shook as sobs racked his

body. His heart felt as if it had broken into a thousand pieces. There were four distinctive nailing moments, each separated by a short period of silence. Each time the pounding began, a new wave of tears fell down his cheeks.

Another loud thud shook Simon from his sorrowful state. This was not the sound of a pounded nail, but the sound of the cross being raised and dropped into its vertical resting place.

Beyond his will, Simon slowly turned to see the scene. Jesus's cross had been erected between the two thieves. Simon was horrified to see Jesus was hanging from the cross only by his arms. Regret for looking rushed over Simon, yet he was not able to turn away. In shock, he covered his mouth with his right hand and watched as two soldiers grabbed Jesus's feet and placed his left foot on top of the right. A third soldier placed the point of a long nail on the center of Jesus's left foot and pounded it through both his feet, into the foot block near the bottom of the cross.

Could he appear any more pathetic? What had he done to deserve such brutality? Naked, bruised, beaten, tortured, with a crown of thorns piercing his head, and now stretched, and nailed through each palm, each wrist, and his feet one atop another with a single massive nail through both.

A depth of sorrow Simon had never known swept over him. He wanted to fall in agony upon the ground, tearing his cloak, and throwing dirt on his body and face. The inability to help Jesus and alleviate his pain felt like a tightening clamp on his heart. He wanted to break through the throng, fight off the guards, take Jesus from the cross, protect him, and tend his wounds. Yet, there was nothing he could do. So, in sorrow, he observed the man he did not know—he who had somehow changed his life.

— — —

Either to mock Jesus or as a jab toward the people who desired Jesus's death, the soldiers placed a wooden plaque at the top of Jesus's cross. It dubbed Jesus the King of the Jews. Local leaders were infuriated by the sign and demanded it be removed.

"If you want it removed, do it yourself," replied the centurion.

They looked at the centurion with disgust. As if to say, "How dare you suggest we defile ourselves with such a task."

In the meantime, three soldiers had concocted a brew, which smelled of vinegar and gall. They soaked a cloth in the mixture, wrapped it around a pole, and raised the cloth to Jesus's lips. Upon tasting the liquid, Jesus lightly shook his head and would not partake.

The soldiers enjoyed offering the bitter liquid. It was obvious they found it delightfully fun and humorous. Seasoned by the military, battle, and death they found entertainment where commoners would be appalled. After much prodding and failed attempts to convince Jesus to partake of the soothing balm they had prepared for him, they decided to offer it to the thieves.

One desired to quench his thirst despite the bitter taste. As the soldiers wagged the cloth in front of his face the condemned man snatched at it with his teeth. A couple of times he managed to catch the cloth and sucked on it as much as he could before it was yanked away. All the while the soldiers were encouraging, taunting, and laughing at his attempts to grab the cloth.

The other condemned man, after seeing the humiliation made of the other criminal, like Jesus, refused to partake.

While the two soldiers were making sport with the vinegar, the others set about having their own fun. From a pouch hanging on his belt, one pulled out some dice and challenged the others to a game of chance.

"And what will be the prize?" asked one soldier.

The instigator grabbed Jesus's undergarments.

"What better prize than the clothing of the King of the Jews," the soldier exclaimed with a snicker.

Drawing out a dagger, one soldier said, "There are nine of us. Let us even the odds."

He snatched the cloth away and cut it into four pieces.

"There," he said, "four lucky winners."

"Let it be five," said another as he held up Jesus's cloak. "This will be the grand prize."

The centurion looked on with indifference, allowing his men to have their fun. He glanced at Jesus with an expression that asked, "So, you're the King of the Jews? Not very impressive."

Jesus's eyes were filled with sorrow. He bowed his head and in a quiet voice that spoke of the treatment and mocks he had sustained, he said, "Father, forgive them, for they know not what they do."

Chapter XIII

-|-

Thirty-One Days Before
Tuesday, March 3—5:30 am

Looking at the sleeping boy, Simon was for the hundredth time, overcome with immense feelings of love. This was his first-born. Never had he imagined so much love could fill his heart. He would do anything for his son. He would stand with him through all trials and challenges. He would defend, protect, and support him in every way possible. Because he was so invested in his life, he would also discipline him when necessary.

Simon understood the responsibility of raising children. He was accountable for their proper upbringing. It was his charge to teach them right from wrong, work ethic, respect, responsibility, and the ability to choose wisely. The duty was not easy. Many times, Simon wondered if he was raising his boys correctly. He often reflected on what he could do better. He questioned if his own example was good enough for them. Once or twice, he considered whether he spent too much time away from home. He was concerned for the day when his boys would choose to follow his teachings or choose a different path. Would his sons be benevolent to their own families and beneficial to their communities? Would they choose to waste their lives away? Would they choose to be a force for destruction and fear? Would they carry on the legacy he had created and continue to expand trade? It was Simon's greatest hope they would be capable, respectful to their wives and children, and honest, dependable leaders.

These uncertainties often plagued him. At times he wished he could decide everything for them, to set them on the best path, and not have to worry anymore. But then he would recognize the injustice of a forced life. They had the right to become their own masters, to follow their hearts, pursue their hopes, and go after their dreams. All Simon could do was raise them to the best of his ability and hope his efforts directed them onto the path of becoming honorable men.

In his own life, Simon had grown to understand the great blessing of discipline. Though not always easy to accept, he was grateful for the moments and people who had molded him into the man he had become. He recognized life was a continual path of learning and growth and as such he would continue to change with each new phase of life. Each stage taught him something new and something he needed at that time. Whether in his childhood, during his apprenticeship, with his work, or as a husband and father, discipline was a consistent valuable instructor.

One lesson Simon struggled with was the skill of disciplining, especially those close to him. It was not difficult in regard to employees, for their appropriate conduct was essential in his operations. Plus, if needed, he could always release them of their responsibilities and sever contact with them. Never had it been a challenge to find someone eager to fill a vacancy. On multiple occasions, probationary action was what retained valuable contacts and improved the behavior of his employees. Simon's efforts to morally and ethically guide those he supervised gained him the status of a respected employer, one who was seen as trustworthy, loyal, fair, and dependable.

However, when it came to his family, Simon could not dismiss and replace them like an employee. For this reason, he considered discipline a double-edged sword. Leniency meant letting his children be taught by the world; a school keen to raise people bent on pride, deceit, gain, and treachery. On the other extreme, being too strict alienated him from his boys. Somehow, he had to find a way to walk the center of the sword. For Simon, this was a precarious path, not easily traveled.

"He'll be fine," said Julia, as she wrapped her arm around Simon's waist.

Simon glanced at his wife and naturally wrapped his arm around her small yet strong shoulders.

"I think I was too hard on him," Simon replied. "Look at him, he is still a boy."

"Perhaps, but he is becoming a young man. It was necessary to prevent such slothful actions. I think you handled it properly."

"I do hope so."

Simon took one last look at Alexander and then turned into the adjacent room to make his final preparations before leaving. Julia followed behind him.

Rufus, who had not been able to sleep that night, had risen early to prepare his things for the journey. He was hobbling about as Simon and Julia entered from the bedroom. Rufus wanted to prove he was capable of going. He had dreamed about his first journey with his father ever since Alexander had the opportunity. He was determined his injury would not make him stay behind.

He and Alexander had only been playing when the accident happened. Rolling boulders down the gorge behind their home had always been one of their favorite activities. They liked how the rocks tumbled, crashed, shattered, and created a rumbling echo through the canyon.

A month prior, they had discovered a new precipice from which to play. Alexander had found a perfect boulder, large, and mostly round. The boulder was heavy and half-buried in the ground. Both excavated the prize, in great anticipation for its exciting descent down the gorge. The size and weight of the stone required the unified strength of both brothers to push it over the edge.

On the count of three, they heaved with all their might to give it enough momentum to rampage down the slope. A rough lip and crag in the rock offered Rufus a perfect handhold from which to push. When the rock's momentum carried it over the edge, Rufus's fingers remained snagged in the crack, pulling him down with the stone. By a miracle, the tumble did not kill him, but the force of the fall dislocated his arm, knocked him out, broke his left leg, and caused a deep gash in his thigh, which had been cauterized.

As Simon and Julia entered the room, Rufus balanced firmly on his uninjured leg trying to maintain the illusion that his left leg was weight-bearing.

"You see father," he said, "good as ever."

Simon was not fooled, having seen how difficult it was for Rufus to move around since the accident. He figured he would play along, but only to help him see he was not fit for the trip.

"You're getting stronger each day," Simon said proudly. Then he asked, "What will you do if we need to abandon ship while crossing the sea?"

Rufus strained to think of something that would assure his father that swimming would not be a problem. An idea came to mind, and he said confidently, "I will hold on to a piece of floating wreckage."

"Brilliant response," thought Simon.

"How fast can you run?" asked Simon.

Rufus's face twisted in concentration. He started slowly as he tried to piece together what to say, "As ... fast ... as ... you can carry me."

Simon smiled at the cleverness of his son.

Julia recognized the helpless expression on Simon's face. She knew it well. For all of his business genius and ability to strategically work with those he dealt with, his own children foiled him often. Simon's attempt to help Rufus recognize he was in no condition to go had been thwarted.

"Rufus," said Julia, "it is too dangerous with your injured leg."

Simon raised his eyebrow at that comment. He was well aware of the possible dangers, but the way she had said it made it sound like something life-threatening would happen.

Julia continued, "The exertion of traveling may make it so your leg doesn't heal properly."

Rufus dropped his head, so his chin rested on his chest. He knew he would not be allowed to go. Two tears rolled down his cheeks. A silent sob shook his small frame. He tried to hold them back, but they escaped despite his efforts.

Simon went to Rufus and knelt in front of him.

"I am sorry, my son. I wish you could come. My first concern is your safety. Though you are nimble on your crutches, the journey is far and difficult. Difficult even for a grown man with no injuries."

Rufus peered at his father, his cheeks wet with tears, and an expression of pure hope that somehow Simon would change his mind.

"I promise you this," Simon said, "On my next journey you will accompany me."

"You promise?"

"As long as you promise to let your leg heal."

"I promise. I will let it rest right now." Rufus gave his father a big hug.

Still in the embrace, Simon said in his ear, "I love you, Rufus. Care for your mother while I'm gone."

"You can count on me," Rufus replied energetically.

Rufus let go, turned, and hobbled into his and Alexander's

bedroom.

Simon and Julia heard him set his crutches next to his bed, the ruffling of his bed covers, and the ensuing silence as he fell fast asleep.

In the stillness that followed, Simon collected the last items he needed. Julia assisted by his side. Simon had completely turned his focus to the task of preparing for his departure.

This particular journey was made once a year unless pressing issues or new prospects required his attention. In such circumstances, he usually extended one of his other trips to address the matter. Out of the twelve months in the year, Simon was away from home for at least eight. Growth and wealth were the goals. A life of ease and luxury for his family was the fruit. Simon did not get to spend as much time with his family as he would like, nevertheless he considered his time away a sacrifice for their greater good. Julia and his boys meant everything to him. It was for them he worked so hard, maintained relations with contacts, sought to expand his influence, and traveled to visit the people who ultimately made the business more successful. His family would never want for anything, as he had in his youth. They would never be in the bottom tier of society, as had been the case with his parents.

Simon enjoyed the challenge of creating, maintaining, and increasing his ventures. Already, twelve regions of the eastern side of the Empire had been economically bolstered by Simon's business. To date, fifteen villages had been saved from certain economic destruction. He had been able to transform those communities into prosperous centers of production and produce.

For his current journey, he anticipated adding two new trade routes to expand beyond the borders of the Empire into the far east. For the past two years, he had been seeking to take advantage of trade routes through Jerusalem and Antioch. If all went as planned, his business would become a major player in the spice industry.

After so much time spent with his business, Simon had come to view his work as essential to his life. It had become who he was. He could not live without the challenges, excitement, and benefits he received. All his travels, meetings, and connections made him interact with people who changed his life. Professional merchants, manufactures, political figures, and military personnel possessing valuable insight, taught him to think bigger and broader. They made him more knowledgeable, enabled him to make better decisions, and provided needed information and connections to expand his business.

Over the years, those Simon worked with meant as much to him as the business itself. They were his occupation. Goods and merchandise moved through their capable hands to consumers, and the money gained flowed back to him. If Simon could keep his contacts and employees content, financial wealth beyond his dreams was inevitable.

Simon was an expert at managing relationships. From time to time, he wondered if he put too much emphasis on building those contacts and too little focus on his family. Every day missed in the lives of his sons was a day missed watching them grow. They were learning so fast and, hopefully, turning into the men he wanted them to become. Simon believed he was sacrificing his life for them. They were the perpetuation of his legacy after he was gone. All he did was ultimately for them. Alexander had joined him on a few of his journeys, not for the purpose of spending time as father and son, but to commence his training in commercial affairs. One day, his sons would inherit the business and they must be able to manage it effectively.

A different motivation tugged at his heart when it came to Julia. Every day away from her was a day missed in the presence of his most beloved friend. He had loved her since childhood. He was completely smitten by her beauty. In the years since their marriage, his love had expanded beyond anything he could have imagined. She was his anchor. Each day his goal was to serve her, to make her smile, to alleviate her burdens, to protect her, to let her learn and progress, to tell her how much he loved her, to hear her ideas, opinions, and advice. He wanted to be able to give her anything she desired. Above all, he wanted to fulfill her hopes and dreams.

These desires had not always been part of his purpose. They had entered his life slowly, coming little by little as he was influenced by people he interacted with. Different cultures, traditions, and ideologies from around the Empire rubbed off on him. Simon had a knack for picking up the best parts of different ways of life, which broadened his perspective, enabling him to effectively connect with others and gain their trust. This was perfect for his business but it did not bode well with his relatives and community.

Many regarded his goals, both in business and domestic life, as radical and influenced by heathen corruption. On multiple occasions, family, friends, and leaders sought to sway Simon in what he had come to view as a more meaningful way of life.

"Simon," implored his Rabbi after a visit to Simon's home, "to live life after the manner of the Romans is in violation of our covenants."

This was in response to a gift Simon had received from a dear friend and contact in Athens. The man accompanied Simon back to his home to learn more about Simon, his family, and his background. Having been so impressed, the man gave Simon what he considered a precious gift. Simon, knowing how to make others feel appreciated and understood, graciously accepted the gift. Even though he displayed the gift as a piece of artwork, rather than a religious relic, local religious leaders were incensed he would even accept such a mockery of deity.

Though less critical than his Rabbi, Simon's older brother did not miss an opportunity to jab at Simon's friendship with Gentiles. This was consistently done by implying that Simon had forsaken his traditions and embraced the misguided beliefs of others.

One day, his brother quipped, "Neptune stopped by and said he is done letting you cross his sea free of charge. He demands payment for his protection."

Luckily, Simon and his older brother enjoyed a close relationship. Though his brother liked poking fun at Simon, he did so in a playful manner. Simon found it a fun game to play. Others were more critical.

With Simon's father-in-law, the situation was completely different.

He argued, "How long do you think you can live the life of two men; one of the covenant and one of the world? You must choose the path of God, otherwise, my grandchildren and my daughter may be lost. Their fate is upon your head."

While on his deathbed, Simon's first employer told him, "You have done well for yourself, but your decision to enter into contracts with those not of the covenant worries me. You are no longer the timid apprentice I once taught. You have become wise and capable in your trade. However, do not allow the corrupt desires of the Gentiles to canker your soul."

The onslaught of critical judgment against his choices caused Simon great concern. One evening, early in their marriage, Simon asked Julia, "Do you think I err in my endeavors?"

Recognizing the humble tone of his question, she answered, "You show greater love and kindness toward me than my father ever showed to my mother, or my brothers to their wives."

"That's not what I mean."

"Isn't it? You worry that your dealings with those not of our faith will shame you. Shame me. Yet, you have learned good characteristics from those you work with and incorporate them into your life. You trust my opinion. You ask my advice. Your tender acts of service toward me are unceasing. Perhaps you should take the men of this town on your journeys so they may learn as well."

She never said she approved of his business, she only said she agreed with the kind of man he had become through his work. That was enough for him. From that day forward Simon never doubted his course. In time, he began to see that his unorthodox views, actions, and relations brought great joy to his family. With Julia, he noticed their connection grew stronger and their love deepened beyond his expectations. With his employees and contacts, he saw great friendships formed and lives changed.

From time to time, leaders and family would question his dealings, but never again did he allow himself to question if his course was correct.

— — —

"That should do," Simon said, tying off the last strap on his satchel.

He slung it over his shoulder and walked the few steps to the front door.

"You're sure you have everything?" inquired Julia.

"Yes," he said resolutely. Then slyly, seeking an explanation for her earlier comment to Rufus, "But I have nothing for unexpected dangers."

Julia said with a sharper tone than Simon had expected, "Don't joke about that. You know I've been unsettled about this trip."

"I'll be careful," said Simon, acknowledging the concern in her voice.

To ease her mind, he asked, "Shall we take a morning stroll?"

Julia smiled. She quietly walked over to the boys' room and made sure they were sound asleep, then went to Simon and clasped his hand in hers.

"Lead the way," she said.

Simon lifted the latch of the door and led Julia outside. Julia closed the door behind her, giving it a little wriggle to make sure the inside latch fell into place. Side by side they descended the stone steps in front of their home and went out into the street.

Simon turned, leading them toward the northern end of the town.

Chapter XIV

-|-

Day Of
Friday, April 3—9:30 am

$\mathbf{A}$ couple of hours passed. Most of the multitude sat off the road upon rocks or in the dirt, watching the scene of the crucifixion. The ground beneath Simon showed the signs of fidgety feet. If Jesus could not rest from the strains of the cross, neither would Simon rest.

As much as he wanted to be far away, he could not pull himself from Golgotha. Having carried the cross, the short distance to this place, Simon felt he needed to stay to the end. After all, the damage to his reputation was already done. A couple of his contacts had come up to Calvary and meticulously looked over the crowd. They did not look upon Jesus or the thieves that flanked him. Rather, they searched for someone specific. Simon knew exactly whom they sought. When they saw him standing alone, dressed in his blood-stained cloak, their faces disfigured in disgust. With a glance, they told Simon never to speak with them again.

One defiantly shook his head, raised his hands over his head, and lowered them abruptly as if swatting Simon out of his life. He swiftly turned and returned from whence he came.

Another, Simon's first contact in Jerusalem with whom he had been in business for over a decade, wove his way through the people, searching for Simon. When he found him, he approached, aghast.

"Simon," he demanded in a shocked voice. "What hast thou done? Do you not care about your business? Surely you have ruined yourself this day."

Before Simon could answer, the man continued.

"I had to see if the rumors were true. I heard you carried the cross for the man Jesus, who claims to be the Son of God. It is blasphemous, Simon. Sheer blasphemy. How could you? How could you!"

Simon opened his mouth, but no words came.

His friend gaped back and said, "Do not come to me again." He turned and was gone.

Simon considered calling after him, pleading with him, and explaining what had happened. But he kept his silence.

With the sun steadily making its way across the sky, Simon and the others watched and waited.

Religious leaders, entering and exiting the city, saw the sign placed atop Jesus's cross and reviled against him. They wagged their heads at him and hissed with their teeth. They mocked things he had taught. Many frequently challenged him to save himself. They mocked him by continually demanding he come down from the cross. They petitioned him to clearly declare who he was. These were the most unrelenting people Simon had ever seen.

Had they not done enough? Was Jesus's mutilated body not enough to fill their grotesque desires? Was his humiliation of being spat upon, falling in the street, and being crucified naked not enough? No. They wanted more. They wanted him reduced to nothing, exposed as a fraud, completely destroyed and forgotten.

Chief priests, scribes, and council members who had followed the procession remained vigilant in stirring onlookers and passersby to vehemently ridicule and berate Jesus. Time and time again, they said, "He saved others; himself he cannot save." This was said with such haughty pride that it irked Simon to the point that he wanted to grab them and nail them to a cross.

Adding to the tumult, the thief to the left of Jesus began a relentless onslaught of insults and challenges directed at Jesus. As is the case with some condemned men, his rantings were not without a cause. He desired his pain to be removed. He challenged Jesus to not only save himself, but him as well, and to take them down from the crosses.

Jesus did not acknowledge the man. He only bowed his head and closed his eyes as if in deep concentration.

At one point, the other thief raised his voice to rebuke the other.

"Be silent," he said. "Why revile an innocent man. You and I have received our just reward for our crimes. This man has done nothing amiss. Let him be."

Even this reproach was not completely unselfish, for he then implored, "Remember me when thou comest into thy kingdom."

This caused the watching multitude to hush. All wanted to hear what Jesus would say in reply.

Jesus painstakingly turned his head toward the man and said slowly, "Verily I say unto thee, today shalt thou be with me in paradise."

Some said, "See, he is not the Son of God; he expects to die. How could the Son of God be killed by man?"

Others proclaimed, "Lofty ambition of a blasphemous man to claim he will go to paradise."

Chapter XV

-|-

Sixty Days Before
Monday, February 3—9:00 am

Simon sat on his favorite cushion at home, situated in the corner of his office near a window that provided an unobstructed view of the street in front of his home. In the mornings, the sun shone directly through the window offering a comfortable warmth and well-lit location from which to conduct his business.

This morning, Julia had gone to the market to replenish the family's food supply. His two sons had risen early and gone off on some childhood adventure. Simon was left home alone, an occurrence he was grateful for, giving him the opportunity to complete the day's correspondences in peaceful silence. In the solitude, he was able to give his work his entire attention.

He reread the letter that had arrived moments before: another discrepancy between shipping and receiving. The porter who delivered it had just departed to convey Simon's response to the port authorities in Apollonia.

Simon found it appalling how inconsistent some merchants were with shipments. The lead merchant at Apollonia, an employee of Simon, had the authority to handle discrepancies in supplies and merchandise. However, when large concerns arose, he devotedly sought the direction of Simon. Usually, Simon had to deal with situations retroactively as he was frequently away on business. He was grateful this particular mishap occurred while he was in Cyrene. This was the final straw of many last chances with this particular supplier. Luckily, Simon would soon be on his way to Jerusalem and could deal with them in person. Either he would sever relations, or knowing they were in dire need, perhaps Simon would come away owning their operation.

That idea made him happy. Immediately, his mind ran through possible employees who could whip the operation into a well-organized effort. Instinctively, he chose John, a man who had mastered the art of reorganization. John could take the least productive group, remove the ones that held everything back whether logistically or financially, and find the right people to replace them. He was also an expert in motivation. Crews under his care soon became honest and performed at their best.

"Yes, John will be perfect," thought Simon. "I will draw up a purchase contract today."

Glancing out the window, he saw another carrier coming. This was why he loved the location of his office; he could see who was coming before they arrived.

Correspondences came by porters who ran from Apollonia to Cyrene. The best and most athletic, who Simon employed, made the one-way trip in an hour and a half. After delivering their message and receiving a reply, they would descend back to Apollonia in just over an hour. With the carrier system, Simon remained accessible. At the same time, he was far enough away that anything not urgent was handled without him. For that Simon was very grateful. He preferred the larger more expansive aspects of business, rather than the daily details of discrepancies, correspondences, and record-keeping; these he happily delegated to others when possible.

Many wondered why the mastermind behind a massive trade

operation preferred to live in Cyrene, rather than at Apollonia or a larger port. It was a question Simon often heard. It was a question he never answered. He refrained from replying, not because he did not like the reason or because he was too proud; he did not respond because he did not need to answer. Regardless of the small town he lived in, he had built a more successful business than most who lived in the influential hubs. This was due to his diligence in personally building relationships abroad. Other leaders of industry gave their all until they were wealthy enough to hire others to do the work. Then they relaxed in their prosperity. In comparison, Simon lived to accomplish growth and expansion through his dedicated efforts. His company was as alive to him as his children, and therein lay the true reason why he was still in Cyrene.

This was his home. Cyrene was where his roots were. It was where he had fallen in love with Julia. It was where Alexander and Rufus had been born. It was the resting place of his ancestors. It was where he learned the value of work. It was where he had gained the trust of his mentor. It was where he gained trust in himself. All that kept him grounded was here. Cyrene was a constant reminder that he could succeed and improve. It now stood as a testament to his abilities to defy odds and build what others believed to be impossible.

Plus, it was here that he started his business with a simple medicinal product. To this day, that small production continued to operate.

When Simon was in Cyrene, he spent his afternoons managing a meager production of Silphium. He enjoyed overseeing his fields with five other men from the town. He diligently coordinated the planting, cultivation, and harvest of the plant. This was followed by making it available for medicinal use. Far from a massive production, it did not bring in much money, but it was his first acquisition and held a special place in his heart. It was the seed that enabled the growth he had achieved.

Simon was not one to let others do all the manual labor. Assisting in the field helped him remember the meager circumstances in which he had been raised and provided a strong reminder of the career he had chosen. But more than that, he found the days in the field satisfying. Working in the field built character: it helped him remember that the field did not wait for the cultivator; it would either produce valuable herbs or noxious weeds, depending on the dedication given. It was the same lesson with business: dedicate yourself to the work and it will increase, neglect it and it will fracture and crumble.

Sweaty from his run, the arriving porter delivered a message that had come from Simon's head merchant in Athens. The notification informed Simon that his business was now the official supplier for upcoming and subsequent events of athletic competition. This was wonderful news. Simon wrote a congratulatory letter to his merchant's dedication in pursuing this designation. Simon included instructions to make sure he stayed in good standing with local political leaders and to be ready to supply whatever was needed.

Once the carrier left, Simon pulled out a blank piece of parchment and set about drawing up a contract for the purchase of the fledgling supplier in Jerusalem.

As Simon directed his attention to the task, he noticed a faint holler in the distance. Only the slight turn of his head gave an indication that he had heard it. He did not take his eyes off the parchment, nor did he skip a second as his thoughts transitioned to his hand, through his quill, and onto the blank page.

The cry got closer and more audible, but it was too distant for Simon to know who it was or what they were saying.

After a few seconds, he caught the cry again. This time he recognized the voice. It was Alexander. He did not pay attention to the high-pitched cries because his two boys often came running home with shouts of competition. When Alexander arrived, Simon would remind him that the whole town did not want to hear his yells and to be more considerate to others.

As Simon continued writing the contract, his attention was alerted by Alexander's cries, which were becoming increasingly frantic as he drew closer.

"Help! Father. Come quick."

Alexander's voice was filled with fear. His words came quickly and jumbled.

Simon immediately stepped out of his home and listened for the next shout.

Still out of view, but definitely coming from the backside of the home, Alexander cried out in desperation, "Please, come quickly!"

Without hesitating, Simon dashed around the right side of the house through the narrow alleyway that separated his home from that of his neighbors. His instant action allowed him to see and call Alexander before his son raced around to the front of the home on the other side of the house.

Alexander ran to his father, grabbed Simon's hand, and began pulling him in the direction from where he had just come.

Between pants, he commanded, "Father. Come quick. Rufus is hurt."

Alexander led Simon to the crest of the gorge, east of town. They had to descend a rolling shoulder of the ridge before the steepening terrain offered a view into the depths below. Once they reached a stone outcropping, Alexander pointed to Rufus's huddled body at the base of a steep incline. Simon called to him. The gentle breeze making its way down the canyon and the echo of Simon's shout were the only audible sounds. He called again, but Rufus did not stir.

"Alexander," Simon said, in that fatherly tone that instantly exclaims the seriousness of a situation, "Run and get Jacob. Bring him here."

Simon had a vast knowledge of production, shipping, markets, sales, negotiations, and diplomatic orders, but he knew little when it came to injuries. Jacob, Cyrene's medical physician, was the one person in the region Simon trusted to help.

Before Alexander had time to turn and go back toward town, Simon had already begun his descent toward Rufus. His feet could not move fast enough. He ducked under a few tree limbs, leaped over decaying logs, slipped down the loose rocks, and somehow managed to keep from falling. Adrenaline surged through his body. His heart pounded.

Despite the loud noises made by Simon's descent, Rufus remained motionless. Instinct, rather than experience, allowed Simon to move nimbly down the steep slope as, with every other step, he called to Rufus. He had not heard a reply. At one point, he had to take his watchful eye off Rufus as he traversed a particularly rocky spot where a misplaced foot would have sent him careening down the slope. After he had crossed the section, he looked at Rufus, hoping for some evidence of life. A sliver of relief came over him as he noticed Rufus's position had altered. His legs, which had been slightly stretched out, were now pulled in tight to his chest.

"Rufus," Simon called. "I am coming."

No reply. Simon surged ahead determined to reach him as quickly as possible.

Soon the slope became twice as steep. For the first time, he noticed skid marks—evidence of an uncontrolled fall. With these traces, Simon also noticed splatters of red on rocks and plants. This caused him to stop and peer closely at his son. He saw a pool of blood gathering around his legs and back.

"Please, Father, no." Whether spoken out loud or in his mind, Simon never knew.

The steep slope forced Simon to slow his pace. Each step was consciously placed to ensure stability and to prevent rocks from tumbling down onto his boy. By foot skill alone, Simon would never have made it down this section without falling. Thankfully, a few scraggly limbs and roots offered steady handholds to aid his descent. Being so close to his son but having to move so slow was excruciating.

The last four cubits, before the slope leveled out, were almost vertical. One brave plant clung to the surrounding dirt. Simon maneuvered himself down, holding on to a flimsy branch and an even more precarious root.

"Please hold, please hold!"

The branch proved longer than the root and soon both his hands tightly gripped the small limb for support. He inched his hand toward the limb's tip but the strain on the branch was too much. The plant uprooted creating a small explosion of dirt and rock. He shielded his face from the airborne debris as he fell backward.

Twisting in the air, he put his hands out in a wild attempt to brace for the inevitable impact with the ground. In so doing, his hands received scrapes and cuts from the rocks below him. He skidded to a stop, quickly oriented himself, and scrambled on his hands and knees to Rufus.

Careful to not irritate any injuries, he shook his son by the shoulder. "Rufus. Rufus, can you hear me?"

The boy let out a slow, wincing moan. His eyes were clenched tight as his moan trailed off.

"Rufus, I am here son. I am here."

Simon checked to see if he could determine the extent of the injuries. Cuts and scrapes crossed his forehead and face. His right arm seemed oddly out of place. Both hands were scraped, cut, and covered in dirt. His left sandal had managed to stay on his foot, but the right was nowhere to be seen. Most concerning was the red stain near his leg and lower back.

He gently rolled Rufus from his left side to his back. He tore the hem of Rufus's garments and gently lifted it off his right leg. As the cloth came away it stuck momentarily to the clotted blood, and Rufus began to yell and cry. He tried to push his father away as he curled into a tighter fetal position to protect his leg.

Determined to find the injury, Simon pulled back the matted clothing. He tried to lift it ever so gently but Rufus let out a scream like Simon had never heard and instantly fell silent and limp.

While Rufus lay unconscious, Simon pulled back the cloth, revealing a sharp slab of rock protruding from Rufus's lower thigh. Simon was no physician and did not know what should be done. He was afraid if he pulled the stone out, the wound would bleed profusely. Panicked, he lifted his son in his arms and looked for a way back up to the rim of the gorge.

He could not ascend the way he had come down. He walked up the tributary seeking a place less steep. With haste in his steps, he moved forward, careful to jostle his son as little as possible, and soon he found a ridge that led back to the canyon rim. The heat of the day had set in adding to Simon's physical fatigue. Sweating profusely and having no water to quench his thirst, he began his climb. He tried to go straight up but loose rock and dirt caused him to slide back with every step. He changed tactics and began switch-backing up the slope. This made it a little easier and provided more secure footing, but the effort of carrying his boy quickly drained his energy. His adrenaline had long since dissipated. Simon forged ahead by pure willpower.

Focusing on the ground in front of him, he failed to notice as the steepness of the hillside increased. He strained to maintain traction. All muscles in his feet were taut and pushed firmly into the ground. The effort was excruciating. His legs were on fire. His lungs heaved for air. Yet, he did not pause. Up he continued to climb, slowly making his way back to the crest of the gorge.

At one point, he began to lose his footing. He dropped to one knee while keeping the other leg locked behind him to stop his slide. Rocks ripped through his clothing, gashing his skin but he focused solely on the task of not dropping his boy. Thankfully, when he came to a stop, Rufus remained safe in his arms.

As he approached the rim, Alexander and Jacob came into view. They were at the outcropping where Simon had originally descended. From their vantage point, a ridgeline had obscured Simon's ascent, leaving both wondering where he and Rufus had gone.

Simon completed the last few steps to the top of the gorge and gently laid Rufus on the ground.

Turning, he called breathlessly to Jacob and Alexander, "Over ... here."

Hearing his call, Alexander and Jacob ran the distance to Simon's side.

As they approached, Jacob inquired, "What happened?"

"His leg is badly injured."

Simon pulled back Rufus's garment to show Jacob the injury.

Jacob bent down and inspected the wound. He took a clean cloth from his haversack. With his right hand, he firmly gripped the protruding end of the rock and quickly pulled it out of Rufus's leg. Rufus screamed in pain and again fell into unconsciousness.

Jacob covered the wound, which gushed blood. He wrapped the cloth around the leg and firmly tied the loose ends of the bandage.

While Rufus lay unconscious, Jacob inspected what else he could do. Aside from the scrapes and cuts, he noticed the dislocated arm and a unique bruise on Rufus's leg, which indicated a possible broken bone.

Turning to Simon he said, "Before he wakes up, I'm going to reset his arm."

Simon held Rufus down, while Jacob popped the socket back into place.

"That will be sore but will cause him no issue. We must hurry with his leg. The wound must be cleaned and cauterized. Bring him to my home where we can make him more comfortable."

Simon stooped down and gathered Rufus into his arms. Then he stood and they began their swift return to town.

Later, back at home, with Rufus sleeping on his bed, Simon noticed the sensitive condition of his own knee. He investigated and found a large tear hidden in the folds of his clothing over the knee. Spreading the cloth to look more closely, he found several cuts covered in dried blood.

Chapter XVI

-|-

Day Of
Friday, April 3—11:30 am

Dark clouds had gathered. They came like a clenched fist, squeezing out the light of day. Simon had not noticed their approach. One minute it was sunny and hot, the next a cool breeze accompanied the shadow of the clouds. The stark contrast caused the onlookers to stare at the threatening sky. Their faces expressed the questions that no one spoke out loud, "Where did these dark clouds come from?"

A few devout Jews, taking note of the impending storm, along with the lateness of the day, began to clamor.

"These men," speaking of the men on the crosses, "will not die before the Sabbath hour begins. It is unlawful to prepare a body for burial on the Sabbath, thus their legs should be broken to speed their deaths. This way we may uphold the law and prepare them properly for burial."

Many considered this sound judgment and petitioned the soldiers to break the legs of the crucified.

Simon was appalled by these requests. "These people speak of the law, but their hearts are far from it. Hours before, they were joyous to see these men tortured, beaten, spit upon, and crucified.

They enjoyed the drawn-out death. Now they want this business done. Enough waiting. Kill them now. But not without increasing their misery. No, a spear to the heart would be too simple. Better to break their legs and speed up the slow process of crucifixion. They speak of upholding the law, yet they seek such a brutal death of an innocent man."

Never had Simon seen such a show of hypocrisy. It made his stomach churn.

The centurion debated with one of the more boisterous chief priests. He shook his head and told the religious leader, "Without a direct order from Pilate, the legs of the crucified men will not be broken. Nor will I send one of my men to petition such an order."

The priest looked furious. Simon was sure his fury was not caused by the commander's refusal of the task, but at the disappointing idea that Jesus's death would not be hastened without again petitioning Pilate.

Turning, the priest spoke to a couple of men who, upon receiving the message, hurried away.

— — —

As the outcast of the group, Simon stood with only his feelings, thoughts, and observations to keep him company. He noticed those who were gathered at Golgotha had separated into three distinct groups.

The first group was composed of those who wanted Jesus's death. They were mostly local religious leaders, and they pressed as closely as possible to the crucifixions. As the hours passed, their taunts diminished in frequency, but they continued to watch Jesus like vultures. Any moan caused them to cheer.

"Come down and sit on this comfortable stone," they would jeer. Or "Come down, I will share my refreshing wine to ease your thirst."

When a seemingly significant event took place, such as when the first trickle of blood made its way from Jesus's nailed feet down the cross and onto the dusty ground, they were quick to point it out. They mocked it and held their heads high as if they were the cleverest individuals on earth.

The second group was made of those Simon believed to be Jesus's friends and family. These stood or sat farther away in an effort to distance themselves from the religious leaders. From time to time these friends appeared concerned that the chief priests might turn on them. After all, they were the ones that supported, trusted, and loved the man who the leaders seemed to hate. Mostly, they stood in silence. Together they comforted and bore each other's sorrows. Their tears and mournful actions were in stark contrast to those of the leaders.

The third group consisted of the soldiers. Seven held a defensive semicircle directly in front of the crosses. Three were positioned behind the crosses. Their presence did nothing to stop derision. Their perimeter was not large enough to prevent spit from the determined from landing somewhere between Jesus's waist and feet. Nor did they put any real effort into blocking rocks flung at the accused. The legionaries were as interested in the crucifixions as animals standing in the heat. They were there strictly by order. After the excitement of getting to Golgotha and performing the crucifixions, they had nothing to do but wait—wait to be relieved by another detail or wait until the men on the crosses died. Until then, they stood, sweat in their uniforms, and kept the crowd at bay.

At the fourth hour, Simon noticed two people, a man who was about the same age as Jesus and a middle-aged woman. These two were held in deep respect by those of the second group. Simon watched them walk to the centurion, avoiding the first group as much as possible. The man spoke to the commander, but Simon could not hear the exchange. The officer glanced at the woman, then back at the man, nodded, and stepped aside. He indicated to his men that everything was all right and not to cause trouble.

Curiosity propelled Simon forward. Those watching the scene had dispersed enough that he was able to walk up to the line of soldiers, placing him only a rod length away from the couple.

The woman painfully looked up at Jesus. Her eyes were swollen and red, and as she took in his body, from his feet to his head, new tears streamed down her face. Her vocal cries had long since ended, the energy for them expended. Rather, her frame shook. She closed her eyes and another wave of sorrow overcame her. The man at her side also had falling tears.

Jesus's voice, weakened by exhaustion and dehydration came down in a soothing tone, "Woman."

A short pause ensued to make sure he had her full attention.

She met his gaze. Though her cheeks were glistening with tears, her eyes had a glimmer of hope. This hope was accompanied by an immense love for Jesus and deep anguish for seeing his torn, beaten, and hanging body. By her body language and the endless tears she had shed since arriving, Simon intuitively knew she was Jesus's mother. Simon's already saddened heart broke a little more. He could not comprehend the agony a mother must go through to see her own son in such circumstances.

Once Jesus had gained her full attention, he continued, "Woman, behold thy son!"

Not being able to point with his hand, Jesus indicated what he meant with his eyes and a small nod of his head toward the man by her side.

Jesus then directed his next comment to the man, "Behold thy mother!" Again, he directed his intent with his eyes and a slight nod.

Then Jesus tightly closed his eyes as if a wave of internal pain shot through his body. He inhaled slowly, as if trying to direct the pain throughout his entire body or to distract himself to better withstand the agony. The big breath of air raised and lowered his chest. Before he opened his eyes, the man and his new mother had moved back into the crowd.

Chapter XVII

-|-

Forty Days After
Friday, May 8—1:00 pm

$\mathbf{A}$ gentle breeze rustled the sails overhead. The sun shone brightly, but not oppressively. Simon stood next to the railing and watched as his homeland appeared in the distance off the port side of the ship. He stood as if entranced, watching the land grow in size across the horizon.

The ship steadily approached the coast and soon Apollonia became visible. Before entering the harbor, the wind was spilled from the sails and the ship came to a stop. They waited for the signal to enter and dock.

Simon watched the hustle and bustle. Three ships were making ready to depart. Six ships were unloading. Other ships were moored strategically to use the available space as efficiently as possible. The ship Simon was on waited for one of the departing ships to leave, giving them access to the dock.

Unlike previous times, the bustle of the harbor did not fascinate him. Though he watched the happenings of the port, he did not take note of them. Simon felt as if he had become time itself, marching on incessantly, stopping for no one, and noticing no one. His mind was exhausted from the tumultuous voyage it had been on. That day in Jerusalem had changed him forever.

He had remained in Jerusalem for a week. Each day he sought to meet with contacts. Most made excuses not to see him. On the fifth day, one contact met with him, but only because he had drawn up documents to entirely sever relations. This contact was a true businessman and never did anything without having a document signed. He acknowledged he was severing the original contract, but listed Simon's deplorable actions of carrying Jesus's cross as more than sufficient grounds to cease working together. Simon pleaded with the man to reconsider, making a case for his loyalty, commitment, and the benefits associated with his connections and merchandise.

His contact only said, "Like that blasphemous man, all you claim to offer died on Golgotha."

He handed Simon a small pouch and said, "In recompense for severance."

Aware more attempts to reason were futile, Simon dejectedly left. He traversed the streets with an incoherent wandering. Eventually, he remembered the pouch of money he held loosely in his hand. He stopped, loosened the cinch string, and peered inside. The sum was a mere quarter of the amount listed in the original agreement for breaking the contract. He was not surprised, but it came as another blow to his apparently failing business. His feeling of futility took a large step into the foreboding abyss of depression. Doubt, self-pity, failure, and depression fogged his mind.

At that moment, Simon walked past an alley filled with the homeless.

All who were within the confines of the narrow space were thin and haggard. Their clothing threadbare, torn, and tattered. Their bodies were filthy. Many stared at their hands or feet, but their focus was completely absent. There was a void in their stares as if all hope had ceased to exist within them. They were breathing, yet life had left them long ago.

Instantly, Simon felt his situation was nowhere near as desperate as these destitute individuals. His heart was pricked and he felt an urge to help in some way. Without thinking, he walked to the first person in the alley, an elderly man sitting against one of the walls. As Simon approached, the man lowered his eyes. Simon crouched in front of him, but the elderly man did not look at him. Then Simon noticed an item that was very much out of place. On the ground next to the old man was a leather satchel. Simon knew it well, for it was his own.

Simon had searched all over Jerusalem for his satchel. He had gone to the local garrison and asked if it had been taken there. After all, the soldiers had stripped it from Simon when he was compelled to carry the cross. No one knew anything about it.

Brutus, the garrison commander, was tolerant of Simon's presence. Though he believed Simon was innocent in the events with the crucifixion, he recommended Simon not come to him for some time. "Let things calm down," he said.

He checked with the shop owners that lined the streets where he had carried the cross. They knew nothing of his satchel but once they found out he was the one who had carried the cross, they became very interested in his experience, which made Simon feel like an oddity only good for curiosity. They cared nothing about the innocence of Jesus or the ruin that had come upon Simon. They only wanted to know the gory details.

He had approached the chief priests but was reviled and cast away before he could even inquire of them.

Now, crouched in front of a homeless old man, Simon had found his satchel. Simon tilted his head to the side and saw the tattered edges of one of his contracts sticking out from underneath the man. He glanced deeper into the alley and saw two other contracts also being used as sitting mats.

Simon was not sure what to do. He had walked over to the

man based on an urge he felt to help. Oddly the urge felt familiar, almost like the warmth experienced when in the presence of a good friend. No words came to Simon's mind. The warmth he felt made him disregard the contracts and satchel he had searched so diligently for. The feeling prompted him to the pouch of coins in his hand. He looked at it, a glimmer of a smile crossing his face. He reached out, took the elderly man's hand, and placed the pouch in his palm.

Simple instruction fell from Simon's lips. "I trust you will distribute this in the best way."

The old man stared at the pouch in his hands. As the cinch was already loosened, he could see the coins inside. What was insignificant to Simon was significant to this elderly man.

Glancing up for the first time, the man looked to see his benefactor. However, as soon as Simon had placed the pouch in the man's hands, he had stood and walked away. The elderly man scanned the street, but only saw the people he saw every day hustling by, avoiding eye contact, and keeping their distance.

Overcome with gratitude, he shouted in his frail voice, "Thank you!"

This drew glares from passersby. Their countenances confirming their belief that the homeless were indeed lunatics. Some of the impoverished acquaintances in the alley were curious and wanted to know the cause of such gratitude.

The aged man observed those he knew so well. They sat huddled and dirty, with hunger evident in their complexions. A slight, almost indistinguishable, flicker of hope ignited in his eyes. He stood, turned, and walked toward the food market, knowing for the first time in a long time, the bellies of those with whom he shared the alley would be full of food when they lay down to sleep.

— — —

$\mathbf{A}$s Simon walked away from the alley, he thought he heard a faint, "Thank you."

He was distraught by the realization that his endeavors in Jerusalem, his biggest and most profitable hub, were in ruin. Nevertheless, at the sound of that "thank you," a smile began at the corners of his mouth and widened the farther he walked. His smile made him think of the things he had been taught over the past couple of days. Those teachings replaced despair with optimism. For the first time since carrying the cross, he was not worried about the future. He knew he could cultivate new relations and build anew. It would take a lot of work, but he was up for the challenge. This time his purpose would be refocused.

Simon had learned a higher lesson in wealth. Gain would no longer be for his legacy, but for the legacy of others. He realized his business had not brought him the joy he experienced when he gave the old man the pouch of coins.

He knew he could do more than give simple handouts. With time and recovered success, he was determined to aid everyone he could. He would build opportunities, help people rise to their potential, bring hope, purpose, and fulfillment to lives. Aelius and his village would be the starting point for this new direction.

Without realizing it, he had begun walking swiftly, and as his mind grasped at the possibilities of using his business to help others rather than to profit selfishly, he became more and more excited. Things he had never considered, avenues of opportunity that could broaden his reach and expand possibilities, played themselves out in his mind.

How could I have been so focused on gain?!

His excitement caused him to do something he had not done since he was a child: Simon began to skip.

Only three joyous skips occurred before he became self-conscious. Pedestrians and shoppers at roadside vendors were gawking at him. Simon remembered the cross, the severed contracts, and the anguish of soul he had felt moments before. Awkwardly standing in the middle of the street, aware of where he was, he instinctively knew this was a life-changing moment. He stood at the crossroads of returning to the somber situation of his failed business or deciding to take a leap of faith and fully embrace the bright possibility that had been born in his heart and mind.

A memory flashed. Simon smiled. He exclaimed, "Just like the young boy from Nazareth!"

This solicited more confused looks from the bystanders who obviously regarded Simon to be out of his good wits. After all, what grown man skips around and exclaims incomprehensible things?

Simon did not concern himself with their judgment. His smile only grew. He knew what he would do. He would be for others what Jesus had been for him many years before.

Chapter XVIII

-|-

Evening Of
Friday, April 3—5:00 pm

$\mathbf{F}$ollowing the events at Golgotha, Simon walked the streets of Jerusalem. He no longer felt like himself. He was confused, worried, distraught, filled with wonder, exhausted, and hurt. Such a maelstrom of emotions shot through his body that he did not know how to react. One minute he was so tense and filled with disgust and anger that he wanted to cause utter destruction to everything around him: smash doors, overturn tables, throw down awnings, and rip canvas coverings. To his satisfaction, the earthquake felt earlier had done all of that for him. He was even delighted to see consternation on the faces of local religious leaders, as he heard them speak about the veil of the temple having been torn in two.

However, the next moment he wanted to huddle in a corner, weep, disappear, and be freed from the torment he felt about his social standing. But immediately, his thoughts would change again and he could not help but be in awe of what he had experienced.

Not knowing how to handle these emotions, he walked and walked and walked. The physical motion of his steps was the only soothing balm to his troubled soul.

Eventually, he ended up at the inn where he had arranged to

stay. The innkeeper, a long-time friend, greeted him with a warm embrace despite Simon's blood-stained clothes. This was the first act of kindness Simon had received from anyone, other than Jesus, all day. It caught him off guard and released a torrent of emotions that completely overpowered him. He clutched his friend's cloak and sobbed while his friend held him close. When Simon's sobs ceased, his friend guided him to a vacant room in the inn. He had Simon sit on a cushion and told him he would be right back. Simon remained there feeling nothing, except emptiness.

Within ten minutes the innkeeper returned carrying a bundle of new clothing. He crouched down in front of Simon and held them out to him.

"Here my friend, let's get you cleaned."

Simon looked at his friend with tears in his eyes. "I have lost everything."

Compelled by emotion, he continued speaking. Topics of his work, family, contacts, sorrow, travels, convictions, failure, wife, confusion, distress, and the crucifixion fell from Simon's mouth in no particular order. Before he finished a complete thought, he began speaking of a completely different topic. To a stranger, Simon's words would have been incoherent, the sorrowful rant of a madman. But the innkeeper understood. He recognized the differing emotions behind each statement and the necessity of letting Simon release them through words.

As the innkeeper listened, he wiped the blood off of Simon's arms and hands. In the process, he noticed the multiple slivers Simon had received. Once cleaned, he set about removing each sliver. He then washed the wounds with a healing ointment.

The discomfort of having the wooden splinters removed did not faze Simon, nor did it interfere with his jumbled explanations. If anything, it caused him to say and express more.

Eventually, he had nothing more to say and he sat with his head bowed in silence.

The innkeeper waited a few minutes to ensure Simon had expressed all he needed to say, then calmly called his friend by name: "Simon."

He called him by name again to make sure Simon looked at him.

"Simon, you are not disgraced."

He took one of Simon's hands and brought it forward and placed the new clothing in it.

"You carried the cross of the Son of God, the Messiah, our Redeemer. You are blessed because you were chosen."

Simon's expression was blank.

The innkeeper was not sure Simon fully comprehended.

"I'll bring you a warm meal."

He left again, leaving Simon to his thoughts.

Simon had a fitful night. He slept, but rest did not accompany him. Nightmares from the day's events plagued him. His dreams were snatches of the events from his journey coupled with the horror of the crucifixion. A ship caught in a storm of reviling men whose words were the wind that tossed the ship to destruction. A stone quarry cast into darkness and then the rocks rumbled, fractured, and fell in all directions. A cross turned nearly upside-down, Simon flailing to get away, but strong hands lashing him to the cross. His contacts dressed as chief priests and scribes placing his contracts beneath the cross and lighting them on fire.

Simon bolted awake, cold sweat running down his forehead. A moment of confusion made him question where he was. Then reality came crashing down. Jerusalem, the crucifixion, his lost contracts.

The room was dim. A sliver of light came in from a tiny window on the wall. Arising from the bed, Simon noticed a basin of water on a low table nearby. He cupped his hand, dipped it in the cool liquid, and proceeded to drink handful after handful. He then splashed the water on his face and wiped it off with a cloth that had been folded and placed nearby.

Glancing out the tiny window, he realized it was still evening.

A gentle rap at the door caused him to turn.

The door opened and in walked the innkeeper with a candle and a plate of food.

"You are awake," he said. "I figured you needed the rest. Here, have some dinner."

Simon was confused. This seemed all too familiar. Had he not just eaten dinner?

"What day is it?" inquired Simon.

"The Sabbath has ended," answered the innkeeper.

"Then I slept through a whole night and day?"

"You did. Though not calmly."

"I don't know what to do. My life is ruined," said Simon mournfully.

"Start by eating," encouraged the innkeeper. He set down the plate, noticed the basin of water was nearly empty, and said, "I will get you more water."

Simon ate ravenously, which exhausted him. He lay down on the bed and was asleep before the innkeeper had returned with more water.

— — —

The next evening Simon returned to the inn after a day of disappointing attempts to re-establish relations with his contacts. Most would not even see him. His attempt to locate his satchel at vendor shops had also been unfruitful. Tomorrow he would continue his diligent search. For now, he was too discouraged to do anything more.

Aside from the demoralizing events of his day, a myriad of rumors was going around that Jesus's body had been stolen, that angels had been seen, that the dead had risen and were appearing to many. Some even said Jesus was alive.

Upon arriving at the inn, the innkeeper greeted Simon warmly. Noticing Simon's despondent countenance, he accompanied Simon to his room.

"Don't give me food," said Simon. "I do not have the stomach for it."

"Tonight, I have food of another kind for you," said the innkeeper. "There is a fresh basin of water and a towel. Clean up and come to the front door when you are ready."

He exited, leaving Simon to himself.

Curiosity drove Simon to heed the command of his friend. Removing his clothes, he washed his body with the cloth and water. He redressed and walked out of his room, into the lobby, and to the front door.

The innkeeper was conversing with a few other guests in the street when Simon exited. Seeing him, the innkeeper begged the pardon of his guests and walked over to Simon.

"Come, my friend, the hour is getting late."

He led Simon down a confusing entanglement of alleyways. Though acquainted with the main throughways and byways of Jerusalem, Simon was quickly disoriented by the many twists and turns. Eventually, they came to a solitary door in a narrow street. Light from oil lamps on the second story dimly lit a window above the door. The innkeeper knocked and the two waited.

After a few seconds, the door opened a crack. A woman stared out at the men with worry on her face. She was perhaps in her late twenties. Her eyes were red and swollen, attesting to a day of tears. She did not recognize Simon but when she saw the innkeeper, her face brightened into a smile and she fully opened the door.

"You came," she said. "Your presence is a welcomed warmth."

To Simon, the excitement with which she greeted them did not match the sorrow he seemed he read in her eyes.

She looked at Simon inquisitively. A glimmer of recognition crossed her brow, but she could not place from where she might know him. She was about to ask, when the innkeeper said, "He is one of us."

This caused Simon's eyebrows to raise in question.

The woman led them into the apartment. The room they entered was small. On the left was a hearth for cooking and a small area for meal preparation. On the right was a doorway covered with a cloth that led to another chamber. Simon heard a few hushed voices but because of the drape over the doorway could not see how many were inside. Just past the hearth, at the back of the room, was a staircase cut into the wall leading to the floor above.

The woman indicated that they were to go upstairs.

"I will not join you," she said. "My heart must relish the joy of the day."

Again, Simon's brow furrowed. Joy was not a word he had expected to hear.

With a big smile and calling the woman by name, the innkeeper said, "Thank you, Mary."

They made their way up the narrow steps, which entered into a single upper room. Seated on cushions near the center of the floor were a man and a woman. The man's back was to the staircase so Simon could not see his face, but Simon instantly recognized the woman.

The man, whose back was to them as they entered, turned. He first saw the innkeeper and instantly stood, walked over, and embraced him.

"Oh, my friend, I am glad that you have come."

The innkeeper pulled away and said, "I have brought someone to meet you."

He stepped aside and motioned with his hand toward Simon.

"John," said the innkeeper, "this is Simon. He ..."

John cut him off in a very respectful and grateful tone, "He who carried His cross."

John stepped forward and embraced Simon.

"My brother," he said. Tears filled his eyes. "My brother."

— — —

Hours passed. The moon made its way across the heavens and dipped below the horizon, leaving a dark sky filled with innumerable stars. The four sat on cushions around the low table. Oil lamps lit the room.

John, and his new mother Mary, spoke of Jesus's life, his teachings, and deeds. From time to time, Mary added her motherly perspective and testimony of the things discussed. Intermittently, the innkeeper would attest to having witnessed some of Jesus's actions, and hearing his teachings as well.

Simon gave them his complete attention. Time did not matter. Sleep had fled from his desire. Though there was a chill in the night air, Simon felt a warm burning in his soul.

At times he rejected what he heard. How could a man change water into wine, calm a turbulent sea, feed thousands with only a few loaves of bread and fish, or even rise from the dead? Though his mind reeled in protest against such things, his heart remained calm. This was the same stillness he felt when he had peered into the eyes of Jesus. This peace convinced him that these things must be true. Not only did this feeling reassure Simon of the validity of what was spoken, but he remembered receiving a conviction while carrying the cross that Jesus was capable of saving himself.

"More important than the things He did, were the things He taught," said John. "Love for all mankind. Service to those who stand in need. Forgiveness for all who have wronged us. Repentance for our sins. Diligently learning and following God's will."

"My heart wants to believe," said Simon, "But I do not see how all these things can be."

"God tests us, Simon," replied John. "He wants to know if we will follow Him even when we cannot see. It is the principle of faith. It is not about completing a list of tasks or obeying blindly. Faith is about seeking to know God, to align our lives with His, and allowing Him to guide us. Little by little, He helps us become more like Jesus. Over time we too begin to acquire the characteristics of heaven."

That jogged a memory. Simon said, "Characteristics of heaven. That is what I saw."

"What do you mean?" inquired Mary.

"There was a moment carrying the cross when I looked directly into His eyes and I saw all that was good and wholesome, complete understanding, and kindness. They were the characteristics of heaven."

Simon nodded his head. Finally, he said, "I believe. I do not understand it all. Yet, I believe He is the Son of God."

"That is the beginning of faith," said John.

To elaborate, John spoke of a father who traveled a great distance to bring his lame child to the Master.

This story resonated with Simon. "Do you know where this father had come from or his name?"

"I do not," replied John. "I heard it rumored he came from the borders of the Mediterranean, but that was only hearsay. Why do you ask?"

"When I arrived at the port in Caesarea, my administrator reported such a story, which has caused quite a commotion among the population. Most considered the man a lunatic for all his boasting about the healing. Nevertheless, his son has been healed, a fact that cannot be overlooked."

Eventually, the oil lamps began to dim. Mary said, "We have

kept you long enough."

She arose from the cushion. As she did, so did the three men.

Mary thanked the innkeeper and Simon for coming and motioned toward the stairwell.

The innkeeper said, "It is always a privilege to be in your presence. Please let me know if there is anything I can do while you are in town."

Simon likewise gave his respects. "It has been an honor to meet you. Blessed be the day when our paths cross again."

"Our paths will cross again," said Mary. She said it without any question of doubt.

As the men went to leave, mother Mary extinguished the oil lamps and lay down on one of the cushions to go to sleep.

The men exited down the stone steps with John trailing behind. The room below was dark, lit only by the glowing embers of the hearth. The young Mary lay asleep on the stone slab in front of the warm hearth.

The adjacent chamber was dark, its members also fast asleep.

John quietly escorted the innkeeper and Simon to the front door. After opening it and stepping outside, John bid the two men farewell, thanking them for their visit. Once they started toward the inn, John slipped quietly back inside, closing the door behind him.

The two walked in silence. The only exchange came from the innkeeper, directing Simon this way or that as they returned to the inn. Simon was deep in thought, pondering the things he had heard.

The innkeeper, aware that Simon would need time to process all he had learned, simply left Simon to his musings. He was ready to answer any question if one was posed but did not solicit the questions he knew would come.

Chapter XIX

-|-

Day Of
Friday, April 3—1:40 pm

By the ninth hour of the day, a menacing darkness loomed in the sky. A cool breeze made its way across the landscape, and all directions lay under the blanket of thick cloud.

Simon thought it interesting these clouds had not brought any rain or even a tempestuous wind. They simply materialized. It seemed to be the Earth's sorrowful response to the happenings at Golgotha.

For the people gathered on the hill, the gloominess of the atmosphere had a quieting effect. Many left not wanting to be drenched by the rain that appeared so imminent. Others left out of boredom. With fewer bystanders, the scorns also decreased. In fact, nothing had been said for a while.

Simon did not notice how quiet it had become, or how long the silence had lasted. The cool shade from the clouds, the calming effect of the breeze, the exhaustion of standing for hours had all quieted the scene. Even the two thieves had simply bowed their heads and now hung in silence. Every now and then a moan was audible, but those groans of discomfort and pain blended in with the surrounding glumness.

Suddenly, a questioning cry pierced the air. Its tone of sheer torment fell from the lips of Jesus as he looked heavenward.

"My God," he said desperately, similar to the way a lost child would cry out in search of their father or mother. His swollen eyes, one of which was so bruised and black that it was barely open, searched the sky as if to see an actual being.

Many looked questioningly at Jesus and followed his gaze up toward the clouds to see if someone was there.

Again, Jesus cried out, "My God." Though his face was still directed upward, he had closed his eyes. Tears rolled from the corners of his eyes as he finished his question. A question spoken with more heartbreak than Simon had ever heard, "Why hast thou forsaken me?"

A tremble shook his body, a body that could not properly express its sorrow from being stretched upon the cross. More tears flowed, dropping to the ground.

This sorrow was different. Former expressions of grief had been directed toward the crowd, loved ones, or the soldiers. The torment that shook Jesus's body at this time seemed to be from a complete sense of loneliness.

By the way which Jesus had voiced his cry and how earnestly he had looked heavenward, Simon was convinced Jesus really believed God had been by his side, but for some reason, God had abandoned him.

Obviously, many other bystanders did not come to the same conclusion.

A clamoring began among the people. Many asked, "What did he say?" Some taunted Jesus saying, "Thou are a madman." Others tried to quiet everyone by proclaiming, "Let him be. He calls for Elias to come save him. Let us see if Elias comes."

Upon hearing Jesus's words, a young man, who stood with those in mourning, ran and retrieved a reed and a sponge. Asking around, he was able to acquire a small vial of vinegar, which he poured on the sponge. Attaching the sponge on the end of the reed he ran toward Jesus.

As the boy approached the cross, the soldiers moved to block his way. The young man was not deterred and ran into one of the guards in an effort to get past. The soldiers' firm stance and grip on the boy prevented him from slipping by.

With this scuffle unfolding below him, Jesus said, more to the soldiers than the young man, "I thirst."

The guards, who had been nearly silent after Jesus asked God to forgive them, glanced at one another, then at the centurion who gave a nod of approval. They stepped aside, allowing the young man access.

He raised the sponge to Jesus's lips. Unlike when the soldiers had done so, this time Jesus placed his lips on the cloth and sucked at the bitter liquid.

"What made this young man's offering any different than that of the soldiers?" questioned Simon. "For in one situation, Jesus refused to partake, while now he accepted. Possibly because the legionaries did it mockingly, while the young man offered it as a means of assistance. Though vinegar is a bitter liquid to drink, it does possess a slight numbing quality."

Then another idea struck Simon. "Perhaps it was because the boy came to aid Jesus in a moment when he felt so alone. The simple kindness of offering a bitter drink may be a heaven-sent comfort in such a horrific moment."

After one more sip on the sponge, Jesus nodded to the boy in gratitude. The young man lowered the reed and slipped back across the road to be among the mourners.

Jesus's eyes followed him, then swept across Golgotha, and on toward the horizon. He traced every hill, ridge, and valley. He seemed to enjoy the view, as if nature itself brought him great joy. Simon believed he was simply taking in the region he knew so well. Like taking a tour of your home before you leave it for the last time.

Next, he looked upon those still gathered near the crosses. The bystanders who sought his destruction, those eager to see his death, and those who fervently mocked him did not make eye contact. They glanced at the ground, at the clouds, or at each other in an effort to innocently miss his gaze. Yet, as soon as Jesus's eyes passed over them, they turned upon him with their detesting glares.

"Odd," thought Simon, "those who had no shame in taunting and mocking him, cannot bring themselves to meet his eyes."

When Jesus looked to those who mourned for him, they made sure their eyes locked with his. In a matter of seconds, whole conversations seemed to transpire between each one. Simon could see Jesus was strengthening them as Jesus had done with him. He was expressing his gratitude and love to each. He seemed to know each one personally. From the expression on some of the mourner's faces, Simon guessed they were shocked to see how personally Jesus knew them.

From Jesus's perspective, he saw all with a deep sense of love. To those who mocked or had beaten him, his stare was stern, but with such compassion as if to say, "I do not hold you accountable, as long as you repent of your ways." Had they only glimpsed what his eyes said, they would have known they too had a friend on the cross.

For those who loved him, his compassion was endless. You could see the deep concern and love Jesus had for each of them. Simon watched both Jesus and each individual he looked at to catch a piece of their unspoken conversation. Soon Simon found himself having his own personal conversation with Jesus. Those piercing eyes looking right back into Simon's.

A memory stirred, clear and bright like the midday sun. Simon recalled the moment vividly as if it had happened only seconds before. Simon remembered back to the day when a young man from Nazareth offered him a new cart and wood to replace his broken planks.

Simon's eyes began to tear up. It was he, the young boy who had helped him so many years ago. He was indebted to that boy, the man now affixed to the cross. Unknowingly, Simon sank to his knees.

Right before Jesus's eyes moved on, a voice entered Simon's mind. How could it be a voice, for Jesus did not speak? Nevertheless, the words Simon understood were as clear as anything he had ever heard.

"*All* are in need of help, and thou hast aided me."

Simon bowed his head and wept.

After glancing at the last individual in the crowd, Jesus's eyes again turned heavenward. Everyone noticed a change in him. Though exhausted from his beatings, torment, and time on the cross, Jesus had recovered some strength. It was as if an internal turmoil had ceased.

All watched him closely. Those who had mocked him appeared fearful, uncertain as to what was happening. Those who loved him were hopeful, desiring that he would be spared from death. Even the soldiers had turned and were peering at him.

With his eyes fixed upon the heavens, Jesus said with a loud voice so all could hear.

"It is finished."

This was said in a grateful tone. Not as an expression of thanks, like someone would give having completed a task they were glad to have over, but as a report of a great feat accomplished.

Speaking heavenwards, with a deep sense of respect and a heightened feeling of love, Jesus said, "Father."

Unlike the last time he had called upon deity, this time he said it as if his Father was very close.

"Into thy hands, I commend my spirit."

Upon finishing these words, Jesus's eyes closed and his head bowed. As his head dropped, his chest deflated, and his breath exhaled. All were silent. Watching intently, holding their breath. His lungs did not re-inflate.

The wind instantly increased. The storm that had been holding back its wrath unleashed its fury.

Heaven and Earth both played a role in the tempest. From the sky came gusts of wind, a torrent of rain, along with the flash and crack of lightning. From the Earth came deep rumbles. The quaking was so forceful that those who stood had difficulty remaining on their feet. Rocks tumbled down the hillside, and a loud crash was heard as if buildings inside the city were being torn and shattered.

Neither storm nor quake continued long. Though the sky remained cloudy, the wind and rain dispersed quickly.

The centurion, who had been positioned directly in front of Jesus, was astonished. Whatever thoughts he had were cut short when a detachment of three soldiers came up the road. They approached the centurion and told him they had been ordered to break the legs of the crucified.

Acknowledging their order, the centurion commanded that they should proceed. Each soldier carried a large wooden mallet and approached a separate cross.

The two thieves on either side of Jesus protested, pleading to be left alone. Their cries were to no avail, nor did they generate any pity. In unison, the two soldiers heaved their mallets and swung them forcefully against the side of the men's knees.

The shouts of the one on the left were silenced by the shattering impact of the mallet as he instantly lost consciousness. Somehow the one on the right remained fully alert. His screams, which were desperate before, now became the most horrific sound Simon had ever heard. Many covered their ears in an attempt to shut out the awful cries.

With their knees broken, the full weight of their bodies hung by their lashed arms. This dramatically reduced their ability to breathe, suffocating them in a short time.

The third soldier, who had walked to Jesus's cross was confused. Jesus made no protests as the thieves had done, rather he appeared lifeless. The soldier nudged Jesus on the leg with the mallet. No response was given. He raised the mallet and tapped Jesus's cheek. No response.

"Commander," said the soldier. "This one is already dead."

The centurion approached and looked up at Jesus.

"We must make sure," said the centurion.

He called one of the other soldiers.

"Romulus," he commanded, "Pierce his lung."

The soldier immediately complied, raised his spear, and completed the quick, well-trained piercing motion. As his spear exited Jesus's side, it was followed by a stream of blood and water.

Those who had come to witness the death of Jesus were satisfied and pleased to see the blood and water spill out. Many smote their chests as if to say, "We told you so. He is not the Son of God, nor the King of Israel. He was only the blasphemous man we said he was."

They left Golgotha as if an ordinary day was coming to a close. No regard was given to the extraordinary man on the cross; no consideration given to the unleashed tempest and quake that shook the earth. "Coincidence," claimed some. "The expression of God cleansing the earth of the man's lies and toppling the man's following," boasted others.

In contrast, the centurion who had been commanded to oversee the crucifixion nodded to the confused soldier still holding his spear.

"He is dead," said the centurion. "Take him down."

Then more to himself, as if to confirm the thoughts he had been pondering moments before he said, "Surely this man was the Son of God."

Chapter XX

-|-

Forty Days After
Friday, May 8—2:30 pm

Walking down the gangplank, Simon's spirits soared with each step. Finally, he was getting off the ship. At last, he was almost home. He could not wait to see his children. Even more, he could not wait to see Julia and tell her of his experiences. She had been right. His journey had changed him.

Once his feet met the dock, he turned and made his way toward solid land, though not very swiftly. Two lines had formed. One made its way toward land; the other led back to the ship. Sailors were carrying gear and supplies on and off the ship. With so many on the dock, it made for slow moving.

Soon Simon had made his way to the wharf front. He glanced to his right and did a double-take. Julia was waving her hands and briskly walking toward him. Her face beamed a loving smile. Simon directed his course toward her.

"Something must be wrong," he thought. This was the first time she had ever met him at the docks. "How could she have known I would arrive today? I am returning a week earlier than originally expected."

Soon the two were standing face to face.

What are you doing here?" inquired Simon. "How did you know I would be here?"

"The strangest thing happened. I could not sleep all night. I had the distinct impression I needed to go to the docks. I didn't know why. The feeling was so unyielding I had to heed it. So here I am, and now I know why!"

Simon wanted to snatch her up in a deep embrace and press his lips to hers. However, local culture looked down upon such public displays.

They looked into each other's eyes. Their smiles increased with each passing second.

"Simon, there is a light in you I have not seen before," she said.

His face beamed an endearing message of love and joy.

"My love, I have much to tell you."

Epilogue

-|-

Sunday, June 24—12:10 pm

The day was warm and bright. The rainy season had ended, and spring had returned. Fields of Silphium, with their vibrant yellow flowers, were in bloom, their sweet fragrance filling the air. Birds chirped. And if one listened closely, they could hear the buzzing of busy bees. The day was a perfect spring day.

But this day was different. Though many crews were out harvesting crops, Simon's small fields were devoid of any laboring hands. Local employees, the new port official of Apollonia, friends, and family had all gathered in Simon's home.

Simon lay in his bed; another coughing fit having just subsided. Julia, well-aged like her husband, sat by his side patting his fevered forehead with a cool damp cloth.

His breathing was heavy and labored. The internal illness caused him to scrunch his brow in pain.

Julia re-soaked the cloth, squeezed out the excess water, and patted his forehead again. The cool sensation caused Simon's closed eyes to flutter open. A moment of blurred vision ended, as his focus settled on Julia. The corners of his mouth raised in a slight, but entirely grateful smile.

He had long since lost track of the days. He could not have said what month it was. He was not delirious; it was just he had been confined to his bed for many months. His frail body was now a shell of what it once had been. His head was nearly bald and the hair that remained was gray. Wrinkles crossed his face testifying to his age, experience, and a life of hard, dedicated work. His tired yet loving eyes focused on Julia, and thus did not notice the family and friends who were also gathered in his room.

In a quiet and hoarse voice, Simon said, "My love."

He was interrupted by a coughing fit.

After it subsided, he continued, "My love, I will wait for you in the kingdom of our God."

Tears rolled out the corners of his eyes and onto his pillow.

On his last breath, with his eyes surprisingly bright and clear and a childish excitement on his face, Simon said, "He is here! Christ is here."

Simon's eyes closed. How grateful he had been to be the one chosen to carry Jesus's cross. After all these years, he would walk with Him again.

The End

About the Author

Tyler is a husband, father, outdoor enthusiast, admirer of history, and loves the challenges of creativity. As a writer, artist, and photographer Tyler works to bridge ideas, depict beauty, ignite curiosity, and tell stories of the heart – more about who people are on the inside, rather than what eyes perceive. His love of historical events, cultures, and people led him to complete an undergraduate degree in History with a language minor in Portuguese and French. He believes the lessons of the past are pivotal to our progression today. With the present always at hand, Tyler loves to slow down and experience the beauty of the Earth. From mountains to canyons, deserts to tropical climes the grandeur of the outdoors is his recharge. You will find him and his family hiking, skiing, camping, and exploring the fantastic wonders of nature.

To learn more, visit his website at TylerGMower.com or scan the QR Code on the back cover.

A Simple Ask

If you found this story to be wholesome and uplifting,
please share it with others!